Whose dark or troubled mind will you step into next? Detective or assassin, victim or accomplice? Can you tell reality from delusion, truth from deception, when you're spinning in the whirl of a thriller or trapped in the grip of an unsolvable mystery? You can't trust your senses and you can't trust anyone: you're in the hands of the undisputed masters of crime fiction.

Writers of some of the greatest thrillers and mysteries on earth, who inspired those who followed. Writers whose talents range far and wide—a mathematics genius, a cultural icon, a master of enigma, a legendary dream team. Their books are found on shelves in houses throughout their home countries—from Asia to Europe, and everywhere in between. Timeless books that have been devoured, adored and handed down through the decades. Iconic books that have inspired films, and demand to be read and read again.

So step inside a dizzying world of criminal masterminds with **Pushkin Vertigo**. The only trouble you might have is leaving them behind.

THE PIERO DISAPPEARANCE CHIARA OF SIGNORA GIULIA

PUSHKIN VERTIGO

Pushkin Vertigo
71–75 Shelton Street
London, WC2H 9JQ

Original Text © 1998 Arnoldo Mondadori Editore S.p.A., Milano

Translation © Jill Foulston 2015

I giovedì della signora Giulia first published
in Italian by Mondadori in 1970

First published by Pushkin Vertigo in 2015

0 0 1

ISBN 978 1 782271 04 8

Text designed and typeset by Tetragon, London

Printed and bound by CPI Group (UK) Ltd, Croydon CR0 4YY

www.pushkinpress.com

THE DISAPPEARANCE OF SIGNORA GIULIA

ONE

Corrado Sciancalepre arrived at his office around midday. He'd been in the magistrates' court acting as a witness in a trial for theft that had taken up much of his time during the past year and was now slowly winding down. The evidence had been weak from the start, but the culprits had finally been identified and the stolen goods recovered.

He was blessed with a special form of intuition, that peculiar mental agility that enables great policemen to delve into the minds of criminals. His successes had mounted up, and a well-deserved promotion was in sight. And yet he would have hated to leave the small town of M—— in northern Lombardy. For ten years he'd been commissioner for public safety, and his two children had been born there. By now he was completely at home in the area and had even mastered the dialect. Locals treated him with reverential respect, almost a prerequisite for his success, and he was particularly well loved by petty criminals. He instinctively knew how to treat them, so that they almost enjoyed being caught by him. In Neapolitan dialect – more familiar to him than his native dialect from Palermo, since he'd lived in Naples at the start of his career – he'd say, 'What's the big deal? I like criminals well enough!' He was born for the criminal as the hunter for his prey.

Outside of his work as an investigator, Sciancalepre busied himself reconciling married couples and putting their kids back on the straight and narrow – a worthy if unglamorous sideline. You could almost have called him an institution. There was no party or meeting – at the home of the mayor, the chief of the carabinieri, the head of finance or the town's movers and shakers – to which he wasn't invited with his wife, a plump and jolly woman from Bologna.

That morning in court, a little gang of thieves had been defended by the lawyer Esengrini, known within the region and beyond as the most agile and authoritative criminal lawyer around. He'd been honorary vice magistrate for around twenty years, was a former mayor, and during the fascist period had been respected and feared as chief magistrate.

Esengrini had spoken little during the hearing. He'd let the reading of the charge and the cross-examination continue without interrupting to question the witnesses, and without a single objection to the public prosecutor or plaintiff. He only asked the victims to clarify a couple of things, because during the summing up it was easy for him to play down the facts and obtain trifling punishments, with the full benefit of the law.

Though lacking the eloquence of a southerner, Esengrini was nevertheless a superb lawyer, worthy of the court of assizes, where in fact he had appeared many times in trials of great importance. He stayed in the area because he loved its peacefulness, but also out of a sort of gentlemanly laziness, one of his most striking characteristics. Sciancalepre admired him unconditionally, and whenever Esengrini read and analysed one of his reports he knew that none of its subtleties would go unnoticed.

Esengrini's personal prestige was acknowledged by the police, the judges and his colleagues, right down to the man in the street. His figure, tall and robust, contributed to this, as did his pallid, severe face, with an old-fashioned moustache and deep-set eyes. But above all, he had complete confidence in applying the most accurate and indisputable legal form to every criminal offence. His authority only stopped with his wife. Twenty years younger, she treated him like an old uncle. His daughter, only just fifteen, thought of him more as a grandfather than a father.

The moment he entered his office upon his return from court, Sciancalepre found a phone message directing him to the provincial capital to confer with the chief constable. He phoned his wife, complaining bitterly about having to miss his daily spaghetti, and set off. When he returned to the police station in the early afternoon he found Esengrini waiting for him; he'd been there for the last half hour.

Sciancalepre was dumbfounded. It was the first time the lawyer had set foot in his office. He immediately sat down at his desk, knowing that it must be something important – something personal – and prepared to listen respectfully.

Esengrini glanced at the door to make sure it was shut. Then, suddenly bewildered – a look Sciancalepre would never have expected on such a noble face – he leant over the desk before beginning.

'Sciancalepre, I'm faced with an incredibly serious matter. It's most upsetting – it's going to turn my entire life upside-down.'

Big words, thought the Commissario. This was new, and unusual coming from a cold fish like Esengrini, someone so reluctant to indulge in confidences.

A short pause, and the lawyer went on, his voice even softer, his face lowered right over the table. 'My wife, Commissario!

My wife has run away from home.' He straightened up, sighing deeply, and looked at Sciancalepre, as if asking him to account for this flight.

'Your wife? But how is that possible? Signora Giulia! Why would she run off, with a husband like you, a daughter, and a house like yours? What the devil are you telling me, Esengrini? I'm very sorry, but I'm afraid I just can't believe it.'

'She's fled. Disappeared,' the lawyer repeated, trailing off tragically. 'Come and see for yourself!'

The Commissario followed him. Along the village road lined with grand old houses, they came to an enormous door that bore the name 'Esengrini' on an enamelled nameplate set up high. The lawyer opened a small door set into the larger one, lowered his head and entered, followed by the Commissario.

They went directly to Signora Giulia's bedroom, which was next to her husband's. It was a complete mess, but not the kind of mess thieves usually leave. It was less hurried, and confined to two drawers; the bed, strewn with clean linens; a wardrobe, left open; and a large, half-empty suitcase – tossed aside, perhaps, for a smaller one.

'As soon as I got back from the trial this morning,' Esengrini began, 'I went to my office to give the typist a few things to do. Then, since it was midday, I came straight home, because today's Thursday. As you know, it's the day my wife takes the two o'clock train to Milan to visit our daughter who's in boarding-school at the Ursuline Convent. For about a year now we've been eating early at home on Thursdays, since my wife has to get to the train on time. This weekly journey to Milan dates back to the time our Emilia went away to school, the same one my wife attended as a girl. I've never been that happy about it, but I didn't dare put my foot down. My wife leaves at two and comes back at 7.30. She visits our daughter, sees her dressmaker, her milliner and, if there's time, does some window shopping on via Montenapoleone.

'This morning, as soon as I went off to court, my wife packed her bags, two of them: a large one and a small one. She didn't go out by the door that opens onto the road, since Demetrio, the gardener who sort of looks after things for me when I'm away from my office, would have seen her going by. She couldn't have gone off on foot with those suitcases – she'd have had to call for a taxi to carry them. Demetrio's usually in the entrance hall, and would have noticed her through the glass door.

'So it's my opinion that my wife went into the courtyard with the suitcases and then down the stairs that lead to the grounds, where someone was waiting for her. She crossed the gardens, went out by the gate leading into the countryside and got into a car. She didn't leave on the two o'clock train – I've already checked. She clearly planned this escape, because I heard her from my room last night, moving around continually, opening drawers, shifting chairs. She was agitated. And I noticed it this morning, too, before going to the office.

'But for some months, Thursday's been an odd day. My wife has to leave, to remember all the things her friends have asked her to do in Milan, put together a packet of sweets for the nuns, keep in mind the things our daughter has asked for, and who knows what else.'

11

The Commissario looked around, shaking his head. When the lawyer had finished, he asked him point blank, 'What else do you want to tell me?'

Esengrini led him into the sitting-room, settled him in an arm-chair and in an altered tone of voice – lower, almost ashamed – added, 'Sciancalepre, you're a southerner and can understand certain things better than I can. I can't say that I'm not up to it, but I'm definitely getting there. In recent years, our twenty-year age difference has really created a gap between my wife and me. Did you notice that even though our rooms are next to each other, they're separate? It's been like that for more than a year. Signora Giulia wants nothing more to do with me in bed. She says that for me, bed is a branch of the office: I read trial proceedings, take notes and look through legal journals until late. I'm sixty, you know, and I'm like any other sixty-year-old man. But my wife is only thirty-eight, to be exact…'

'So?' asked Sciancalepre.

'So one Thursday four months ago, I had her followed to Milan, and something turned up for me – though to be honest, not much. Sergeant Arcidiacono, you know the one who was employed here and who's been at police headquarters in Milan for six months? He did the job for me. He followed my wife and reported to me for two Thursdays in a row. As soon as she arrived in Milan she'd hurry through the visit to our daughter near the Ursuline in half an hour, then go to sit in the tea room at the back of a little pastry shop on the corso Monforte where – guess who was waiting for her? That engineer, Fumagalli, the young guy who was around for a while last year while he was

12

working on enlarging the harbour. He became part of our circle, remember? You too had him at your house. He was our wives' little pet. Yours invited him to have tortellini with you. The magistrate's wife wanted him to marry their daughter, and Commendatore Binacchi's daughter, the older one, seemed to have reeled him in with her dowry of half a million.'

'I remember, I remember,' said Sciancalepre, nodding slowly, his eyes closed. He zoomed through his memory, his policeman's intuition bent on finding some sign of the young man.

'It was definitely Fumagalli. They were chatting and drinking tea. Once, he took her hand gently.'

'And then?' asked Sciancalepre.

'Then: nothing. When she was trailed the second Thursday, they left one another after tea and she took a taxi. Arcidiacono hopped into another one and followed her. My wife's taxi stopped in viale Premuda. The sergeant stopped there too, but just at that moment there was an attempted robbery in a little jeweller's, and he had to intervene. So he lost my wife.

'That's it. I didn't want to go on looking into it. I decided to wait until the end of my daughter's school year to take away my wife's excuse for the weekly visits to Milan. And I determined to take her on a long cruise in the summer in order to work on winning her back – all unlucky husbands have the same false hope.'

'Esengrini,' Sciancalepre began, 'I'll start looking for her immediately. But I'll need you to bring an action against her.'

'Ah, yes, that. Let's see, what should I charge her with? Abandoning the marital home, don't you think? It's the only possibility in this case. I'll send it to you before this evening.'

'Tomorrow I'll go to Milan to look for Fumagalli,' said the Commissario. 'Let's see what he has to say.'

They stood up. Sciancalepre wanted to be taken round the park, up to the gate and along the path Signora Giulia would have used in the first part of her escape. He already knew where the house and gardens were, but he saw them now in a new light. He made a note of the way the façade of the old villa Zaccagni-Lamberti, where the Esengrinis lived, aligned with the other buildings on the via Lamberti. The front door opened onto the street, and a bit further along was the door to the lawyer's office. Set into the façade were two barred windows, one corresponding to the study and the other to the entrance hall. From the entrance a short corridor led to a larger hall-way, off which opened three rooms that had been turned into archives, each with windows onto the internal courtyard. At the end of that hallway, a solid door led to Esengrini's quarters, arranged over two levels of a wing that stretched about twenty metres into the grounds; looking out over the gardens was a spacious balcony. Opposite this was another parallel wing, in line with the house on via Lamberti. Signora Giulia's parents had lived in that part of the house until ten years ago. At their death, the apartment had been shut up and was now awaiting renovation – perhaps when Signora Giulia's only daughter got married.

Between the two wings was a courtyard with a fountain at its centre. A balustrade marked the boundary between the house and the grounds, and from the balustrade a double staircase descended to the park below. The gardens stretched about two hundred metres from the house towards a tall gate that let onto a country road. The grounds were surrounded on all sides by high walls that bordered the grounds of the nearby Ravizza and Sormani houses.

On his way out of the house the Commissario went through the office and asked the gardener, Demetrio, to come along with him. At the station, he questioned him briefly. Demetrio verified that on the morning in question, Signora Giulia had not left through the study or through the front door in via Lamberti. Sciancalepre knew that Demetrio's wife had gone as usual to the house that morning to help with the chores, and that she'd been sent home almost immediately on the pretext that since Signora Giulia had already made the beds, she could return later to do the cleaning.

One could therefore place Signora Giulia's departure at some time after eleven, and through the gate at the edge of the grounds. The key to that gate was normally kept on the ground floor of an old coach house standing against the park wall. Esengrini had already confirmed that the key had been left in the keyhole on the inside, and the gate left ajar.

Since it had been dry for several weeks, Sciancalepre thought it pointless to attempt to take impressions of tyre marks from the country road running alongside the gate – all the more so since at least ten cars passed along that road every day on their way to the lake.

TWO

Next morning Sciancalepre took the train to Milan. Huddled in a corner of an empty carriage, he thought about Signora Giulia and tried to put himself in her shoes.

His glasses slid down his big nose, the colour and shape of cooked macaroni, and his eyes, caught by the ads in the first-class carriage, roamed over the luggage racks, across the seats, from the corridor to the windows. It was almost as if they were guiding his sensitive nose in every direction, like a gun, all over the cushy seats, which had so often held the soft shape of Signora Giulia, aiming to discover the secret of her disappearance.

As soon as he arrived in Milan, he set out to find Fumagalli. He was in his office, in a building in the town centre.

Fumagalli recognized the Commissario right away and welcomed him warmly. He remembered Sciancalepre's wife's tortellini and those evenings a year ago when the beautiful local women had swarmed around him. The Commissario realized immediately that Fumagalli was not connected with the disappearance of Signora Giulia, but he interviewed him thoroughly all the same. The young professional had no trouble admitting that he'd seen Signora Giulia in Milan a number of times. In fact, he made it clear that he'd encountered her for the first time at the station a year before, when he'd invited her to have tea with him. From then on, for many Thursdays, they'd arranged to meet in a little pastry shop on corso Monforte. Their relationship had always been above board; it hardly seemed necessary to say so.

'I liked Signora Giulia,' Fumagalli admitted. 'I had a bit of a crush on her, even though she was ten years older than me. I confess, Signor Sciancalepre, that I was almost in love with her. But Signora Giulia treated me like a boy. She confided in me and once or twice caressed my face, like this,' and here he touched the face of the Commissario. 'She told me she led a sad life, didn't love her husband, and that he neglected her. When I offered her my loyalty and my love, she smiled sadly. In the end, she put me off by telling me she was in love with another man, who unfortunately didn't love her in return. It was someone she came to see every week in Milan, but who didn't care much about her after his initial interest. I've heard it said that a woman in love is an impregnable fortress, and when I realized that that's what she was, even if her love was unrequited, I began to spread out our meetings, until one day I was vague about the date of our next appointment. From that time on I've not seen her.'

'Did you know,' said the Commissario, 'that Signora Giulia has fled her home? That she's deserted her husband?'

'It doesn't surprise me,' Fumagalli responded.

'You're the only one who's not surprised, because in M——— no one can believe it. And I have trouble swallowing what you've said. I've known Signora Giulia for ten years. I accept that her husband is not the kind of man most likely to satisfy such a beautiful woman, someone so full of life. But Signora Giulia's love for her daughter, and above all her upbringing and deep religious conviction, make me discount the idea of this lover you're telling me about.'

'Well,' Fumagalli insisted, 'she definitely had one. Whenever the clock struck four, she'd leave me in the pastry shop and go off on her way. She didn't even want me to see her to a taxi. One time I watched her get into a taxi and then I asked the driver of a nearby cab whether he'd heard the address she'd given.

'"I think viale Premuda," he said. "That's all I know, if it helps."'

Sciancalepre returned to M——disappointed. The situation was more complicated than it had seemed at first.

Esengrini was waiting for him in his office.

'Unfortunately, my friend, I've ascertained nothing that you didn't know already,' Sciancalepre told him. 'Her meetings with Fumagalli were innocent. A few things remain sketchy, but we'll clear them up.'

Two days had passed since Signora Giulia's disappearance. By now word had got round the district and her scandalized friends were all talking about it whenever they met in private. They were very annoyed that Signora Giulia hadn't confided in one of them; they felt betrayed and started gossiping. Some said the trips to Milan were inexplicable; others accused Esengrini of being too cold.

The parish priest held Signora Esengrini in the highest regard amongst his patronesses, even though she was the youngest of them. He was brave enough to go to the lawyer's house to express his sympathy and to assure him that his wife was an exemplary woman, with nothing on her conscience. Perhaps, he suggested, she'd experienced a sudden and inexplicable crisis. 'Nerves, it's nerves! These are horrible times!'

Sciancalepre, who by now knew more about Signora Giulia's nerves than the priest, settled down patiently to wait for a sign. Wives who run off always provide one after they've found their feet in a new situation. They get in touch with someone they trust and try to re-establish a connection so they can follow not only the lives of their children, but also what's going on where they used to live – somewhere they're sure to have shocked with their actions.

The sign Sciancalepre was looking for came from the least expected corner. On the Monday morning following Signora Giulia's flight, who should appear in his office but the gardener's wife, Teresa Foletti. She was forty-eight and lived with her husband in a lodge across from the villa Zaccagni-Lamberti.

The Commissario sat with clasped hands, as if begging for a telling revelation, while the woman made this confession.

'Sir, I've not slept for three days, ever since the sudden departure of my employer. I have a secret that may not amount to much, but my conscience tells me it's time to reveal it. It's something not even my husband knows.

'About a year ago, Signora Giulia entrusted me with a delicate matter. I've been receiving letters from Milan; in each one, there was a letter addressed only to "Giulia". I'd let her know whenever one arrived, and she'd come to my house to read it hurriedly. After that she'd burn it in my fireplace.'

'How was the address written?'

'By hand – and by Signora Giulia herself.'

'So what are you trying to tell me?' asked the Commissario, his eyes bulging.

'I'll explain,' Teresa responded. 'Signora Giulia told me that her daughter, Emilia, was sending her these letters from school.'

'But she was seeing Emilia every Thursday!'

'Yes, but at least twice a month, Emilia wrote her a letter. Signora Giulia said that her daughter was letting off steam in the letters, something she hid from her father and from the nuns. The daughter offloaded onto her mother. What can I say? The signora explained to me that every now and then she'd leave her daughter a packet of envelopes addressed to me in her handwriting, and an equal number of smaller envelopes with only "Giulia" written on them, also in her handwriting. I assure you that the handwriting is definitely hers. I've always kept this secret, and if I've decided to speak now, it's because the signora's disappearance has left me with an anxiety that I can't explain. I would hate for anything to happen to her! You read such awful things in the papers…'

Sciancalepre had finally scored a point. And the clues were starting to add up.

Two days later the gardener's wife returned to his office, again in the morning, while her husband was busy in Esengrini's office, where he sometimes served as a clerk, sometimes as his right-hand man.

She'd barely stepped into the office before silently putting a letter down on the table. Sciancalepre grabbed the envelope, read the address and looked at Teresa.

'What's this! Another letter?' He looked at it, sniffed it, turned it every which way and read the franking mark: *Rome, 22 May 1955, XII-17.*

'The twenty-second of the fifth month in the year nineteen fifty-five, twelfth postal district at five o'clock. What a lot of fives!' he exclaimed. 'Should have added an eleven – the sign of the cuckold's horns – and divided it by a double set of three – or rather, one of those and a set of four, because an eleven is needed on both sides!'*

Teresa didn't understand this numbers game but she agreed that the Commissario should be authorized to open the letter. Inside was the small envelope addressed to 'Giulia'.

'As usual!' she remarked.

'Is it always the same handwriting?' asked the Commissario.

'Yes,' said Signora Foletti. 'The only difference is that the others came from Milan, while this one seems to have come from Rome.'

At this point the Commissario let Teresa go. He didn't need her continuing presence or her authorization to open the enclosed letter. But before dismissing her, he warned her with all the severity he could muster: 'Not a word about this to a single soul, not for any reason in the world! Understood? Not even to your husband. In fact, keep quiet *especially* with him, or you'll hinder my inquiry. And then there'll be trouble! Trouble for you! Because there's something suspicious here.'

After she'd left, Sciancalepre made himself comfortable and offered up a special thank-you to Santa Rosalia, to whom he was devoted. Then, filled with an acute sense of professional pleasure, he slit the envelope with his letter-opener. Not even when he was young and in love had he opened a letter with

* The common Italian hand gesture symbolizing cuckoldry involves holding up the index and small fingers in a configuration resembling the number 11. The sets of threes and fours refer to the lottery.

such trepidation. A sheet of business paper appeared, written on in a masculine hand entirely different from the one on the envelopes. He looked at both sides of the paper and read the signature – *Luciano* – before beginning the letter with forced calm:

> *Dear Giulia,*
>
> *On Thursday I waited for you until five-thirty. I'm sorry you didn't come, because at the very least I wanted to say goodbye before leaving. But perhaps it's better that we didn't meet. We would have suffered more at our parting. My work has made it necessary for me to move here.*
>
> *Like you, I left the little apartment where we passed so many happy hours with great unhappiness. Now, though, the distance between us makes our meetings impossible. If I should happen to come to Milan, I won't hesitate to write to let you know. We could meet in an inn or a* pensione. *I still have three envelopes addressed by you, to you, and they'll be useful in the event of a trip there one Thursday. For now, I don't have a fixed address because my work is sending me all over central Italy. If I can find a pied-à-terre – not so easy in Rome – I'll mail you the address.*
>
> *With my affection, as ever,*
>
> *Your Luciano*

Immersed as he was in the investigation, and realizing that one never knows where an inquiry will end up, Sciancalepre had already begun withholding from Esengrini the second part of Fumagalli's revelations – the ones about Signora Giulia's

23

mysterious lover. He continued to keep him in the dark about the letters.

In fact, he went to Teresa Foletti's house, ensuring that Demetrio was in Esengrini's office before showing up, and advised her once more – in no uncertain terms – not to breathe a word to anyone about the letters. It was understood that should any more letters arrive, she would bring them to him immediately.

An inspector less shrewd than Sciancalepre would have sat back and waited for another letter to arrive. But the Commissario was a born policeman, and he knew that you must never leave holes in investigations as long as there's the smallest detail to settle. For now, he advised Esengrini to call his daughter home from school.

As soon as Emilia was back, he went to the house to see her. Skirting around the issue, he asked her if she had ever written to her mother from Milan. Yes, she'd written a few letters. But it was easy to establish that they were normal letters addressed to the family.

Now that this marginal and almost superficial line of inquiry was exhausted, Sciancalepre went to Milan. There, with the help of two subordinates, he questioned every concierge on viale Premuda. He would have extended this investigation to buildings on the neighbouring streets, but after two days' work the diligent sleuth's good fortune enabled him to discover that there'd been three removals in viale Premuda in the last two weeks. One of these involved a certain Luciano Barsanti, who worked as a rep.

The concierge at the building he'd left confirmed to Sciancalepre that Signor Luciano Barsanti was a young man of about thirty: tall, sporty – and here she made no bones about it – not lacking in women friends. The doorkeeper (a gem in any police investigation) was able to recall from among Signor Luciano's female visitors a regular one on a Thursday. A beautiful woman, no longer particularly young, would arrive in a taxi at around four in the afternoon and leave again a little before six. Chestnut hair scraped into a bun at the nape of her neck, pale, her figure ample, elegant but not overdone. Obviously a woman of a certain class, since she tried to avoid the doorkeeper's gaze as she passed. She was clearly embarrassed, a feeling Signor Luciano's usual friends demonstrated not in the slightest.

Sciancalepre had no trouble recognizing Signora Giulia from the doorkeeper's description. It stuck with him in the two rooms, still empty, that Barsanti had lived in. He went in full of curiosity and, looking around, spotted an electric light switch dangling against one wall. He inspected the little bathroom and closed a tap at the sink, which was still running with a trickle of water. He found it difficult to bring the visit to an end, fascinated as he was by the invisible presence of Signora Giulia. He saw her moving around the place, imagined her every gesture, each expression. Signora Giulia! His wife's friend, Emilia's mother, esteemed by the priest of M—— for her good works, her kindness and donations… Signora Giulia, with whom he'd danced so many times at friendly get-togethers, appreciating like a good Sicilian her fine, glowing Lombardian health… That sad, sweet face, which the lawyer Esengrini never even looked at, but everyone else admired. In these very rooms!

And Luciano Barsanti? Maybe one of today's youth who carelessly, even scornfully collect the affection and the love of women they can't begin to understand: real ladies, delicate souls seeking a love they fantasized about as girls, and now disappointed by the realities of a bourgeois marriage that's deadened them, confined them to a small provincial town. A young guy who had lots of affairs, a bit offbeat, someone who went for models and women who scream in bed, who'd maybe accepted this complicated relationship with a woman ten years older for some personal gain. Who could tell? Signora Giulia must have given him gifts of silk shirts or pyjamas. The concierge said she'd seen her go up several times with one of those long boxes wrapped up by shop clerks in the town centre. Shirts, pyjamas, ties, possibly a few 10,000-lire notes…

What we won't do to hang on to a relationship that's slipping away from us, an image of fading love. So sad! Perhaps Sciancalepre had done something similar himself… It didn't bear thinking about.

He couldn't get any more out of the concierge that would help him identify Luciano Barsanti. The building manager didn't know anything else either. So he went straight to the town registry office. Nothing. Luciano Barsanti was one of those types who don't register in a new town, but maintain official residence in their native town or city instead. The kind who move from one place to another without leaving a trail in the local records.

Nevertheless, Sciancalepre could imagine Barsanti, and he felt sure that sooner or later he'd put a hand on his shoulder:

'Police! Come along with me, young man.'

26

THREE

Back in M——, Sciancalepre put the results of his busy days
and his trip to Milan on a long list. He added a point to
form an uncertain line snaking across Italy – now towards
Rome – in search of poor Signora Giulia. He always called
her that, poor Signora Giulia, when talking to himself. At
home, whenever he put down his fork after consuming his
daily serving of spaghetti or tagliatelle, he answered his wife's
questions with the same words: 'Poor Signora Giulia! What
was she thinking about? How could she do it? Oh women,
women!' He shook his arms over the table and glanced intently
at his eight-year-old daughter beside him, already fearing
for her future. His own wife didn't worry him; she was close
to fifty and extremely secure after ten years of untroubled
marriage.

But he didn't say 'Poor Signora Giulia' to Esengrini when
he visited him in his office every few days towards evening.
With Esengrini, he spoke only of the undeniably disappointing
results of a search conducted throughout the whole of Italy
with Signora Giulia's photo. Esengrini himself had provided
the photo, and Sciancalepre had a copy pasted on the cover
of the file kept locked in his desk. Each day, when he opened
the drawer, those sad eyes looked up at him, as if begging him
to persevere. *Don't give up*, they said to him, *look for me, don't
lose heart. You'll find me.*

The more the Commissario thought about Signora Giulia's disappearance and the details his investigation had turned up, the less he understood the matter. With whom had she fled? Not with Fumagalli. Not with Luciano Barsanti, at least not according to the letter. Of course, it could very well be said that Barsanti and Signora Giulia had arranged the letter between them, convinced that the gardener's wife would give it to Esengrini – as if Signora Giulia had said indirectly to her husband, *I've got out of there, I'm with a man, and it won't do for you to look for me or start a scandal. There's no going back. Have the separation papers prepared with me as the guilty party. Do whatever you want but forget me, and I'll forget you.*

And yet, it couldn't have been like that. What about Emilia? Was it possible that her mother was no longer concerned about her? Why didn't she at least send a few postcards? Why didn't she write to one or two friends to justify her actions? He closed the drawer angrily, gave the key a twist and got up, restless.

He'd gone back to Esengrini's house many times, looked the place over from top to bottom, around the grounds, in the greenhouse and in the abandoned coach house. There was nothing to offer him the faintest lead.

Meanwhile, the month of July had arrived. By now fifty days had passed since the disappearance of Signora Giulia. One morning, the post brought Sciancalepre a telegram and a large envelope from police headquarters. The telegram couldn't be anything other than the usual reports that did the rounds.

He opened the large envelope. It was the poster sent from police headquarters every year at the start of the swimming season:

'*The Chief Constable calls attention to the police rules and disciplinary sanctions established by the penal code for the protection of public decency. Bathers must refrain from entering the water in residential areas and must wear street clothes in bars, restaurants and other public places. The wearing of bathing costumes is prohibited in the streets, etc., etc.*'

He then opened the telegram and sank down on the wooden armchair; the large envelope containing the poster fell to the floor.

'*Rome, Police Headquarters. Information concerning the search for Giulia Esengrini and Luciano Barsanti: yesterday Luciano Barsanti applied for a passport, giving his address as via Agamer, n. 15, Rome. Awaiting instructions, etc., etc.*'

'Got him!' cried the Commissario, for once renouncing his own dialect in favour of the local one, as if to address the people of M——, who'd been waiting two months for the diligent Commissario to succeed. After a couple of telephone calls to police headquarters and to Rome, he prepared to strike.

The following morning found him on the express train to the capital. *I'm going to get Signora Giulia*, he said to himself. *I'm going to get her and bring her home, if everything goes well.*

Before leaving he'd called on Esengrini with some urgency. 'Sir,' he said, 'we've made some headway. I have reason to believe that your wife is in Rome – with another man, unfortunately, a young guy she's been writing to without your knowledge. I can't put it any other way.'

The lawyer tried to find out more, but Sciancalepre wasn't about to reveal anything. Esengrini took him by the hand and pleaded, 'Sciancalepre, we've known each other for ten years. You know who I am. Tell me what's going on!' But to no avail. The Commissario knew his trade. Yet he felt he had to tell Esengrini the name at least: Luciano Barsanti. The lawyer remained indifferent. It was the first time he'd heard it.

'He's the man your wife's with,' the Commissario explained, 'and if you want to help me get my hands on him, you've got to make an accusation – this time, of adultery. Without it I can't surprise them at home. You know that better than I do.'

Esengrini sat down on the spot and recited to him the charge from the official form:

'The undersigned, etc., etc., having reason to believe that she, his wife, etc., etc., is in Rome, where she is cohabiting with a Luciano Barsanti in via Agamer, n. 15, lodges complaint against Giulia Zaccagni-Lamberti, married name Esengrini, and against her correspondent Luciano Barsanti, requesting all investigations and such verifications as may bring the crime to light in flagrante, etc, etc.'

He made it without hesitation. He wanted to get to the bottom of the matter, move towards a separation and sort out all his dealings with his wife. They'd have to go through the arrest of the guilty and then the withdrawal of the charge (already planned) in order to procure the separation order with her as the guilty party. It was the necessary route, as well as the only possible one. As for pardoning his wife or letting her back in the house, Esengrini wouldn't even think of it, something Sciancalepre noticed.

■

With the charge in his pocket, the Commissario travelled to Rome, looking around at the Etruscan hills as he passed through Chiusi. *Who knows how many cuckolds there were, even in Etruscan times!* he thought. He tried to follow the history of adultery from the time of Adam forward, and came to a single conclusion: that horns had always been the real cause of all evil. In fact, they are at one and the same time the devil's distinguishing feature and the symbol of conjugal infidelity! Could it be any clearer?!

Sciancalepre considered himself a psychologist manqué, and among the various states of the human mind and their multiple reflections in the psyche he claimed to have studied those of unlucky husbands in particular.

'If you think about it, being betrayed is a desirable situation, one that's peaceful, even restful,' he'd say to his closest friends. 'The trouble lies in uncertainty or doubt – when one fears the worst but isn't sure. When you're sure, your fear is at an end. The anxiety fades away and a certain calm takes its place.'

Thinking along these lines, he turned back to Esengrini's problem and asked himself what he, Sciancalepre, would have done in his shoes. *I'd have poisoned her,* he mused, *or shot her on the spot, at the right moment. No one could have argued that it wasn't a crime of passion, and I could get off with a few years.* But he had to reject the idea that the lawyer could kill his wife: he wasn't a passionate man, Esengrini, and he had too great a horror of violence. Killing his wife and getting rid of the body wasn't something he'd do. A doctor could have done it, but not a man who'd always lived by the book.

Upon his arrival in Rome, Sciancalepre went to police headquarters to enlist the aid of a couple of officers, and then made a visit to the area around via Agamer. The road itself started from one of the main piazzas in the suburbs and meandered out towards the countryside. Number 15 was halfway down: a five-storey building full of office workers but without a concierge. Across the road, a space had been cleared for the construction of another apartment building. It hardly seemed like Rome at all. Where was the Colosseum? The Lateran Palace? The Forum? Not having had time to stop in the centre, Sciancalepre felt like he was in a city with no name or history. A wretched, swarming anthill, the place for runaways, wanted men and vagrants.

He looked at number 15's pigeonholes. There it was, the name Luciano Barsanti, on the third one. *I've got him*, he thought. He ran up the stairs to find Barsanti's apartment – third floor on the right – and then looked over the plan for that night.

He was already on the spot by seven that evening, opposite number 15, in an old Fiat 1500 borrowed from headquarters in Rome. Officer Rotundo dozed at the wheel, his driver's cap tilted over his eyes. Behind him, Sciancalepre and Officer Muscariello sank back in their seats, smoking. To pass the time, the Commissario made Muscariello tell him a bit about life in Rome.

Every now and then someone went into or came out of number 15, ordinary people of no particular interest. When it got dark around nine, Sciancalepre had them move the car in front of the building's entrance so he could see who was coming and going.

At around ten, a couple came from behind the car and entered the hallway of number 15. Sciancalepre hardly had time to see the shape of a handsome young man and that of a woman who could have been Signora Giulia. He waited for his heartbeat to settle before leaving the car and going to the opposite side of the road, pretending to look for the best place to take a leak. All the while, his head half turned towards the building, he watched the third floor from the corner of his eye. He saw the lights go on. They were trapped now! He only had to let a quarter of an hour pass by while they got comfortable. And sure enough, ten minutes later in one of the third-floor rooms: a pink light. It had to be an *abat-jour*, a little alcove light.

Sciancalepre felt in the pocket of his jacket for the paper with the official charge and made a move towards the car. He left Rotundo at the entrance and went up to the third floor with Muscariello.

He pressed the doorbell. After what seemed like an eternity, a peephole opened almost imperceptibly, and a man's voice asked, 'Who is it?'

'Police!' said the Commissario, his mouth at the jamb. 'Open up now or we'll break down the door.'

The door opened immediately, and a young man of about twenty-five stood in the opening looking serious and worried.

'Let us in!' Sciancalepre shoved the young man aside. Muscariello followed behind him, his hands in his jacket pockets. Sciancalepre moved the youth between them and pushed the door to. Then, standing in the hallway right under the young man's nose, he said rapidly and quietly: 'Luciano Barsanti, you're under arrest. Come with me to the bedroom.'

His head down, Barsanti led the Commissario towards an internal room. As they got closer a woman stuck her head defiantly through the doorway. Sciancalepre stopped in his tracks and stared at her.

He couldn't stop looking at her, so anxious was he to make up for all the time that had elapsed since Signora Giulia's disappearance, and to come to grips with the changes she must have undergone.

But nothing could have explained such a radical transformation.

Sciancalepre didn't want to admit it even to himself, but this woman wasn't, and never had been Esengrini's wife.

He turned to Barsanti. 'Who is she?'

The woman answered, 'I'm the wife of Fasullo, the MP. What do you want with me?'

Sciancalepre had pulled the charge from his pocket but it occurred to him that as far as this situation was concerned it was just a piece of paper. Sure, it mentioned Barsanti, but it certainly couldn't be applied to this specific case. 'In that case...' he murmured to himself, 'in that case...'

He knew he was in a pickle. He'd rushed into things, albeit with an accusation in his pocket and a watertight warrant. But he found himself to have surprised only one of the accused in a crime not covered by the official charge. *This* crime was being committed with someone else; so it was *another* crime, and not the one specified by the current accusation. And now he had the wife of an MP in front of him! He wasn't sure what to do.

Noting his embarrassment, the woman began to breathe more easily. 'So where are we?' she asked. 'What's Italy come to if you can't pay someone a visit without informing the police?'

'Pardon me, madam,' the Commissario humbly offered. 'I've acted in accordance with a standard warrant. It's just that there's been an error. A partial error, since Signor Barsanti is under arrest and must accompany me to police headquarters. As for you, madam, I can only offer my apologies. Report to your husband, the MP, that there's been a misunderstanding, a mix-up of persons, and that I'm sorry and beg his pardon. As far as I'm concerned, you can go now. Where may I take you?'

'I don't need any help!' the woman screeched, heading towards the door.

Sciancalepre sent Officer Muscariello behind her to tell Rotundo, still guarding the front door, to let her go undisturbed. Then he turned to Barsanti.

'You and I are going to have a few words now at headquarters.'

In an office at the station, Sciancalepre began the interrogation. First of all, identity: Luciano Barsanti, twenty-six years old, born in C—— near Livorno, company rep for colours and finishes, etc., etc.

Then he asked, 'So, you were living in viale Premuda in Milan?'

'Yes.'

'And you were seeing women there as well!'

'From time to time. I'm young…'

'Were you seeing married women too?'

'It might have happened.'

'You're right it happened, young man! You were seeing Signora Giulia Esengrini, and every now and then you wrote her a letter and sent it to M—— in an envelope addressed to Teresa Foletti. I have those letters right here in my hand. Go on, keep talking…'

'What's to tell, if you already know everything? It's true. I met this woman one afternoon on the train between M——and Milan. Then – you know how it goes… we met a few times in a café, struck up a friendship…'

'Go on, tell me about this "friendship"!'

'The first time, we went to a *pensione* I know around via Mario Pagano. Then she began to feel uncomfortable, and I had to find a little apartment.'

'With money she gave you?'

'I don't earn much as a rep. And she was the one who wanted it. I got bored right away, but she was sentimental and said that if I left her she'd throw herself into the lake.'

'Well, lake or no lake, Signora Esengrini has gone missing, and it's your job to tell me about it.'

'Me? But what do I know! After the letter from the lawyer, I gave up the flat and left for Rome. I didn't want any further trouble.'

'What letter?'

'A letter written to me by Signora Esengrini's husband. He told me he knew all about the affair, everything, that he'd had us followed, and it was better for me to leave the area and forget about his wife. You get the drift! I was out of there in less than eight days. The rental contract had expired, so I sold the furniture and cleared out and came here to Rome. Actually, the day before I got the letter from the lawyer, his wife missed our usual Thursday rendezvous for the first time. It's obvious that her husband stopped her coming. In his letter he warned me, "Make sure you don't tell my wife I've written to you!" So I wrote to her acting the dunce. I feigned surprise that she hadn't made the appointment and told her I was leaving for Rome. A few nice lines, to soften the blow…'

36

'Where's the lawyer's letter!' shouted the Commissario.

'The letter? I don't know. I threw it out. You think I'd carry something like that around with me? What good would it do? I throw all my letters away. Even the ones Signora Giulia wrote to me every week.'

The interrogation went on for several hours, and Sciancalepre was convinced that Barsanti was telling the truth. He warned him, for caution's sake, to register any future movements with the police and to make sure they could find him in case he was needed. He recorded the deposition with great precision and then, with these few papers, he disappointedly turned back the way he had come earlier with so much hope.

Now, he said to himself as the train crossed the Apennines, *Signora Giulia seems almost like a ghost. If she didn't go after Barsanti, she didn't go after anyone else. And she definitely didn't throw herself into the lake. She would have left a letter. And one doesn't take two suitcases on a suicide mission… At this stage,* he thought, *I'm going to scratch out the word 'fled' and write 'disappeared' on her file.*

The following morning he went to see Esengrini.

'Wrong track. No trace of Signora Giulia. Barsanti was there, but with someone else. Get this: the wife of an MP! You can take comfort in that.'

The Commissario recounted for Esengrini every last detail of the expedition, and when he got to the bit about the letter, he asked him, 'So you never heard his name, this Barsanti, before I spoke of him to you?'

'Never.'

'And yet,' the Commissario continued, 'you wrote him a letter. He told me himself. Unless he dreamt it!'

'Impossible! It's not true!'

After this meeting, which ended a bit frostily, Sciancalepre realized that his investigation into Signora Giulia's disappearance would have to go down another path – and that Esengrini would not be as cooperative as he had been thus far.

He started by issuing a search warrant in a different tone from the first one. Then he called the gardener, Demetrio Foletti. He ascertained that Foletti knew nothing about the postal services his wife had provided for Signora Giulia and, in an effort to get to grips with the atmosphere in the Esengrini household, he got him to talk at length. But he just had repeated to him things he already knew.

Foletti was a man of about forty, exceedingly loyal to his employers. He'd always been the gardener at the villa, starting when Signora Giulia's parents were still alive. After their death, around ten years ago, he'd begun to make himself useful, during his free time, in the lawyer's office. Fascinated as he was by legal matters, he became something of an office employee. He went on various errands, took phone calls when the typist was busy, welcomed clients, and now and then managed to give his legal views to some who, seeing him amongst all the codes and official forms, considered him to have a smattering of legal knowledge or at least the rudiments of its practice. He moved from garden to office, gradually neglecting the grounds with which neither the lawyer nor his wife could be bothered, and applied himself with better results to the more impressive responsibilities of clerk and trusted employee. It was therefore he who knew most about the lawyer's family relationships, after his wife, Teresa, who'd acted as cook and housekeeper.

There was someone else at the Esengrini's house fairly often, a young girl called Anna who did the washing and other heavy work. But Sciancalepre learnt little from her. He got much more from Foletti, in whose opinion Signora Giulia was a saint and the lawyer a great man. All the same, it had seemed to him that their marriage had been cold and distant. The lawyer was gruff and didn't know how to be affectionate, while Signora Giulia, who'd lost her mother at fifteen, was a romantic who craved affection and understanding. There'd never been any scenes between them, just long silences.

The Commissario learnt from Foletti that the palazzo Zaccagni-Lamberti, as he called it, was an old property in Signora Giulia's family, and that at his death ten years earlier her father had left the house and grounds to his young grand-daughter, Emilia.

The Esengrini Affair, covered at length by all the papers, had run into the ground. The Commissario was intrigued by the somewhat romanticized version of the story published by an illustrated magazine. The journalist hadn't neglected to come up with a few theories about Signora Giulia's disappearance: that she was being held in Milan by someone who'd met her during one of her Thursday rendezvous; that she'd fled abroad with a mysterious lover; or suicide. Sciancalepre hoped that the article, illustrated with several dated photos of the via Lamberti and the park, and a pretty portrait of Signora Giulia and Emilia – who looked extremely like her mother – might fall under the fugitive's eyes. If her eyes were still open on the world… But he was beginning to doubt it, and every time he received a photo of another unidentified female corpse, he studied the features scrupulously, in fear of making a terrible discovery.

After a month, he renewed the search warrant for Signora Esengrini and decided to wind up the case with a detailed report. He then transferred the file to the public prosecutor's office, leaving the conclusion to the legal authorities.

Following a review of the investigation, which could do nothing more than repeat the main questions, the public prosecutor authorized the archiving of the papers relating to the disappearance of Giulia Esengrini, née Zaccagni-Lamberti.

FOUR

Emilia had now left her school at the Ursuline Convent in Milan for good and enrolled in the university. In the autumn she'd begun taking courses there, and she now made the trip to Milan almost every day.

In the well-to-do homes of M——, everyone was still talking about Signora Giulia. She'd become a sort of ghostly presence at the usual gatherings. They talked about her until the spring, when the wound slowly closed over.

Emilia went to all the usual dos at family friends', occasionally accompanied by her father. Sometimes the lawyer bumped into the Commissario at one or another of the houses. On such occasions they tried to avoid each other, and before long, the guests soon understood that it was better not to invite these encounters. Even if they had not, Esengrini thought it over, and after making a few appearances, he stopped going to the gatherings. Instead, he slowly withdrew, also cutting back considerably on his professional commitments. If he'd been considered somewhat gruff before, he soon became known for being reclusive and misanthropic. No one was able to say that his wife had dishonoured him except the Commissario who, though he knew about Barsanti, had kept his mouth shut, even with his own wife. All the same, the spectre of a crime was perhaps worse; inexplicable, but enough to throw a sort of dreadful suspicion on Esengrini.

Emilia, reserved and seemingly indifferent, got on with doing all the things young people of her age do. Intolerant of older people, she kept to a few friends from university who regularly made the trip with her from M—— to Milan, and there she widened her circle a bit more. She went home with some of them to listen to records, happily drank the odd whisky and loved trying out all the new dances.

The last time she'd travelled from Milan to M——, before the summer holidays, she found herself sitting across from a young man of about twenty-eight who said he knew her. She didn't remember anything about him, but he reminded her that two years earlier he'd been at her home and had seen her in the best houses in M——. He finally introduced himself as the engineer Carlo Fumagalli – a nice guy, and very different from her usual university crowd. A bit overbearing and somewhat unprincipled, but attractive.

They saw each other again a couple of weeks later for a game of tennis. Fumagalli stayed in M—— for the entire summer. The sailing club had been given the go-ahead to begin building a small marina and the engineer, an expert in this type of work, was overseeing the work. As a member of the club, Emilia saw Fumagalli continually during the long summer afternoons, and on one of them they went out sailing for a long time with some friends.

As the boat turned towards the harbour, suspended on the last breath of wind, Emilia, seated at the back, leant her head on the tiller, which Carlo was holding, while the others were all at the prow or else halfway down the boat watching the sunset. Emilia felt something touch her hair. It wasn't the wind, which had almost dropped by now… it was Carlo, gently winding his fingers through it. She turned to look up at him and smiled. The boat tacked, and a little later let down its sails in the small marina under construction.

The relationship didn't go anywhere all summer, but just before Emilia began the regular journey to Milan once more, the two bumped into each other one day in the street. Fumagalli told Emilia he'd soon be returning there, and suggested that they could meet some afternoon at a café in via Montenapoleone. Emilia agreed and proposed a day.

They met in the café two afternoons a week. Little by little, Emilia distanced herself from her university friends, becoming solitary and detached like her father. Even in the train, she'd find a compartment at the rear where her companions wouldn't follow her, excusing herself by saying she had a lot to read.

One evening she found Sciancalepre in that compartment. They made the entire journey together, and for the first time, Emilia spoke about her mother. She'd realized by now that there was something strange about her mother's disappearance, and she wished she knew what was in her father's heart. But it was something she'd never been able to ask him because she felt intimidated – or perhaps because she understood it was something they must never discuss.

'It's a mystery. A mystery!' said the Commissario. And he tried to get her to speak, asking what her father thought about it. 'Did you read the papers?' he asked.

'Yes, I read them. But I don't believe any of their speculations. In any case, as far as I'm concerned, my mother's dead: I can feel it.'

Truth to tell, Sciancalepre also sensed it, but he didn't want to think any more about the case. The folder, with the photograph of Signora Giulia fixed to it, was still in his drawer. Formally, the case was still open, but the paper in the file was starting to yellow and surely some day soon one of his successors would send it to the archives. And Sciancalepre was expecting a promotion – which would mean a transfer.

Another spring came along, followed almost immediately by a hot summer.

The marina for the sailing club was now completed, but Fumagalli returned to M—— for his holidays. He spent his days with Emilia at tennis or in the boat, and in the evenings danced with her on the terrace of the Hotel Europa. No one was close enough to Esengrini to be able to tell him how familiar his daughter had become with the young engineer from Milan. But she told him herself in the autumn, after starting her third year at university.

Esengrini started violently, as if someone had prodded him from behind, when Emilia said briefly after supper one evening that she was set on becoming engaged to Fumagalli.

'No.' He was firm. 'I will not give my consent.'

In vain, Emilia insisted that she was serious about marrying. Her father, increasingly obstinate, declared himself absolutely against the marriage. Realizing that it was useless to insist, Emilia stopped talking about it. But she went on seeing her unacknowledged boyfriend. They got together even on Sundays now, since he spent his days off with her on the lake, having settled in the area.

The lawyer didn't find out a thing, though he couldn't be sure that his prohibition was being respected. A wall of coldness had arisen between him and his daughter. They almost never spoke any more, and the few necessary words they did exchange took on the tone of reciprocal lashings.

Once, no doubt irritated by the incessant phone calls his daughter received from Milan, Esengrini said, 'Whoever disobeys me scorns me, maybe even hates me.'

'Why don't you tell me where my mother is!?' Emilia screamed, herself shocked by this unexpected outburst.

After this exchange, the lawyer's house became a tomb, icy and silent. Emilia went in and out as if it were a hotel, and Esengrini for his part withdrew in the evenings, tired and fed up with everyone who treated him with exaggerated respect while whispering behind his back.

Corrado Sciancalepre knew that Emilia and Fumagalli considered themselves engaged, and would certainly marry just as soon as Emilia came of age, when she wouldn't need her father's consent. Probably even Esengrini was aware of his daughter's intention, but he never gave any sign of having changed his mind about a marriage he didn't want to hear spoken about. And in fact, no one did speak to him about it, because it was known that Fumagalli had been seeing Signora Giulia and could in some way be connected with her disappearance. Even Emilia knew it; Fumagalli had told her himself to explain her father's attitude. Naturally, he kept it to saying that he'd known Signora Giulia and that they'd met a few times in Milan – with the result that he, too, had been questioned at the time of her disappearance. But he'd been unable to give the police any leads, since his encounters with Signora Giulia had been casual and innocent. They'd met in a café on corso Monforte where the engineer habitually went for tea at

45

around five and where, by sheer chance, Signora Giulia went too while waiting for the evening train to M——.

By this stage, everyone was waiting for Emilia to announce her marriage as soon as she turned twenty-one, Sciancalepre in particular. He had a funny feeling that this marriage was going to stir things up again, and that something new might surface now, nearly three years after Signora Giulia's disappearance.

The date both feared and expected approached. Emilia turned twenty-one on the 18th of June but already, a month before, she'd begun requesting the necessary papers for the marriage. It was celebrated first thing in the morning on the 21st in the little church of San Rocco, which sits in the hills above the town of M——. No one was invited to the ceremony and no one was forewarned – except for Sciancalepre, who went on a mission to see Esengrini the same morning at the couple's request.

The new couple went away immediately following the wedding ceremony. Emilia had spent several days packing a bag for the journey, which she'd sent to a childhood friend so that she could pick it up on her way back from the church. She put it in the boot of Fumagalli's big car, sat beside her husband and left for a secret destination. A few days later, their closest friends gleaned from their postcards that the couple had gone on honeymoon to Switzerland, to a little hamlet whose very name – Beatenberg – seemed to promise the peace and perfect happiness Emilia craved after the long years of study and solitude with her father. One could see from the postcards that the village was opposite the Jungfrau.

Right after the departure of the two young people, Sciancalepre went to see Esengrini, whom he found in a state of extreme depression. He struggled to get a conversation going.

'This is the second escape, Sciancalepre,' the lawyer said, 'and you had a hand in it yourself this time!'

Sciancalepre explained how Emilia had thought through her decision. And he stuck to the view that under the circumstances, it was the best possible solution, since nothing could be done about the tensions between Esengrini and his daughter, which were by now unavoidable.

Esengrini had known something was going on from the letters addressed to Teresa Foletti by Emilia, and he began to insinuate, in conversation with Sciancalepre, that there must have been a secret understanding between mother and daughter. Perhaps his daughter, if not actually in cahoots with her mother, knew a bit more than he did about her disappearance.

Sciancalepre didn't accept the suggestion. He discussed the situation that had arisen in the Esengrini household and the new reality that prevailed after Emilia's wedding, and made it clear to the lawyer that his daughter intended to take possession of the house and its grounds upon her return from the honeymoon. They were now her property, according to her grandfather's will. In fact, her father's guardianship was nearing an end, along with his administration of her property, by dint of her marriage and coming of age.

When Esengrini had taken in Emilia's decision, he realized that his continuing presence in his rooms had become untenable. He had a month before the couple's return, and he calmly prepared himself to say goodbye for good to the home he'd gone to live in after his own marriage. He bought

47

a large apartment in a new block that rose over the lakeside square and moved there, together with his office, his files and household furniture.

Sciancalepre, following everything in the guise of trusted intermediary for both parties, was in contact with Beatenberg, and when Esengrini had cleared himself and his things out of the old villa Zaccagni-Lamberti, he alerted the couple that they could return.

Fumagalli and his wife came back to M——a few days later, but only for the short time necessary to begin remodelling and restoring the house, in particular the empty wing where Emilia's grandparents had lived. For the time being, they were staying in Milan with Carlo's mother while he went back and forth directing and overseeing the work. The house was ready in a month, and the flat previously inhabited by Emilia's parents was shut up in its existing state, as well as the lawyer's office, which faced via Lamberti.

The renovated apartment retained intact its eighteenth-century furniture and overall style; only the bathrooms were modern. The park was left neglected and was now entrusted to the scant attentions of the good Demetrio, who still frequented the house, even though he'd followed the lawyer to his new office, where he continued to act as his secretary. For her part, his wife entered the service of the new signora, and the rhythm of former times was re-established.

The villa's salons were opened up to guests. On beautiful summer evenings, Sciancalepre went once more with his wife, and so did Commendatore Binacchi with his wife and daughter, by now a hopeless spinster. The neighbouring Ravizza and Sormani families came with their sons and daughters, and the presence of a few young married couples helped to liven things up. At least twice a week, the Fumagalli couple returned the visits, and the life of the small town went back to being as fashionable as its old habits and daring new innovations – television, waterskiing and rock 'n' roll dancing – would permit.

The marriage was the happy result of a love match, and in common with many other young couples the Fumagalli put off having children so as not to bring too soon an end to the carefree life. They were completely absorbed in their happiness, content with the immense house their youthful enthusiasm had brought to life once more, which they were slowly exploring from cellar to attic. They never felt the need to use the grounds. They looked at the park from the courtyard terrace or their balcony as if it were a body of water, fascinating and treacherous. On moonlit nights, after their guests had left, or on returning from an evening with friends, the two young people stood on the large balcony off the master bedroom, facing the gardens. Leaning on the railing, they looked at the old trees lit up with the moon's glow, the grown hedges forming an impenetrable thicket, a few milky white spots on the path between the plants, and the two huge magnolias on the first level under the double flights of stairs, their every leaf glittering.

Autumn had begun and one night, home late, they went out as usual onto the balcony and watched the moon throw its light over a park shrouded in darkness, then withdraw it as it disappeared behind a moving cloud formation. The bedroom lamps were off and Emilia stood silent for several minutes, as if drawn by the shifting moon, before abruptly gripping Carlo's arm.

'Look! Over there!' she said. 'Do you see that shadow stretching along the path?'

'It's the shadow of a branch,' Carlo replied.

'No,' she insisted. 'A minute ago it wasn't there, and the path was completely lit up by the moon. The shadow moved forward while a cloud went by, darkening the grounds.'

Carlo shook his head, smiling. But just at that moment the shadow moved, reappeared farther away, and then disappeared. A moment later he heard the distant crunch of dry leaves under the magnolia, as if someone were cautiously stepping over them. Emilia shivered again and Carlo led her into the room, quietly closing the shutters. She couldn't get to sleep, and only much later did she allow herself to be persuaded that the shadow could have been thrown by a bit of cloud, and that a cat had surely made that sound in the leaves.

Two nights later, after turning out the bedroom lights, Emilia felt like going out on the balcony again. Carlo followed her and found her intently focused on that bit of pathway where they'd seen the shadow two nights earlier. The balcony was dark, since the overhanging eaves hid it from the moon's beams. For at least half an hour it would remain in shadow, invisible from the park.

Though her husband tried to get her to go in, Emilia wanted to stay there till the bitter end, keeping watch below. Eventually Carlo brought her a shawl. As he placed it on her shoulders, he followed her gaze. She started, suddenly more alert.

A black shadow was moving along the path that began at the gate. It came forward, disappeared under an arch formed by branches, reappeared, and again disappeared. Meanwhile, the moon had moved and a band of light now fell across the garden façade of the palazzo. Emilia withdrew, but Carlo remained with the shutters drawn, watching through a crack.

'Anything more?' Emilia asked.

'Not a thing,' he said.

FIVE

After that, Fumagalli hurriedly wound up his business in Milan and a few weeks later established himself in M——, taking on projects he could carry out by working at home, and going to Milan only very rarely.

He was convinced now that someone was prowling around the grounds at night, and he suspected it was more than a petty thief. He'd walked through the trees, checked the lock on the gate – which seemed to have been shut for a century – inspected the railings and the surrounding walls. Not a sign. He hadn't even seen anything interesting in the old coach house along the external wall; on the ground floor, where there were a few agricultural tools belonging to Demetrio, he saw the gate key hanging from a nail. Rusty and covered with old spiderwebs, it had certainly not been touched since it had aided Signora Giulia's escape.

Having made an inspection, he went to tell Sciancalepre about it. The Commissario looked as if he'd been woken from a long sleep. He listened attentively and asked if he could go out on the balcony on the next moonlit night.

A few nights later, just before midnight, Sciancalepre and Fumagalli took up their posts on the balcony facing the park. Emilia had gone to sleep in another room. With a bottle of good cognac and two glasses set out on a coffee table, the two of them cast a glance every now and then towards the moonlit paths. Sciancalepre, fearing the damp, wore his usual black cap pulled down over his eyes. Until midnight he sat smoking, hiding the burning tip of the cigarette in his hand. But he stopped when the hour struck, leant on the windowsill and didn't take his eyes from the path on which Fumagalli claimed to have seen the shadow.

Suddenly he put his right hand on Fumagalli's knee beside him. He'd seen the shadow. He followed it as it appeared and disappeared in the moonlight, until it was lost to sight completely in the bushes in the middle of the park. Not long afterwards he heard the sound of the magnolia's dry leaves in front of the greenhouse. And a quarter of an hour later he saw the shadow again: it stopped in the middle of the path, farther away, and seemed to him to pause there, turned towards the balcony. For a moment he felt as if he were meeting its gaze – the gaze of a man standing down below between the pine and the roundish mass of beech. It headed towards the palazzo like a death ray, making for the balcony and its white curtains, skimmed earlier by the moon, behind which the young newlyweds would be sleeping.

Sciancalepre slowly took his binoculars from his pocket and crouched down by the railing to look through them. Fumagalli also crouched down, because the rising moon had begun to illuminate the façade of the palazzo.

Back inside, they went to sit next to a lamp in a room on the ground floor, taking the bottle of cognac along with them.

'So did you see that it wasn't an optical illusion?'

'I did – and I'd say that in my view your nightly visitor is someone we know well, a rather tall man with a dark overcoat and a black cap...'

'My father-in-law,' Carlo concluded, his voice low.

'The same. And I ask myself what he's doing here in the grounds at night.'

'Maybe he comes out of nostalgia for this place he lived in for so many years,' said Fumagalli. 'Unless he's drawn here for other reasons...'

'He's had enough time in three years to walk around the park,' said Sciancalepre. 'If he's come back, it's for a reason. Tomorrow morning we'll take a closer look.'

Early next morning, Fumagalli and the Commissario went into the gardens. They started by visiting the greenhouse, where Demetrio was preparing to put the azaleas and lemon trees for the winter, and continued into the grounds. They found no sign of footprints on the worn dirt paths, nor did the areas around the gate or the old coach house reveal anything suspicious.

In the coach house, the key was still in its place, covered with spiderwebs. They took their time examining the gate, conscious that if it had been opened, it would have left a semicircular track on the ground. They walked along the walls at the property boundary and reached the gate, where a wooden door opened onto the street from between two flaking pillars. Neither one of them had previously noticed this door, but they were sure that no one could have used it, because the lock was fixed on the inside by a wooden stick that fitted through two joints in the wall. There were no possibilities left apart from the hypothesis that someone had climbed over the gate or one of the park's two boundary walls at the sides. In the latter case, the nighttime visitor would have had to come through one of the two adjacent villas.

While Sciancalepre studied the ground like an old Sioux, Fumagalli looked over the coach house, which was near collapse. It was evidently a place where two or three horses and a couple of carriages had been kept some fifty years ago. On the top floor were two rooms, now missing their shutters, where the coachman had perhaps once lived.

Fumagalli saw that with just a few modifications, the building could be used as a garage for his car. It wanted only a rolling shutter in place of the fence, which had itself perhaps replaced an old door. A circular courtyard, now grassed over, opened out in front of the coach house, and was divided down the centre by a path that began at the gate and went as far as the middle of the park. There, it became two smaller paths in the form of a semicircle that joined up at the grotto created in the hollow at the base of the double staircase.

He could see in a glance how little work was necessary to complete the project; he'd also resurface the path between gate and courtyard with pressed gravel. As for the courtyard, he felt there must be some paving stones under the grassy covering that had sprouted up from the soil. To find out, he took a pickaxe from the coach house and hacked at the ground here and there. All at once an arrangement of old, round paving stones came to light, damp from having been covered up for so long.

Sciancalepre, who'd been walking around all this time, was curious to see the engineer swinging the axe. He came closer. 'What the hell are you digging up, Fumagalli?'

'I was just looking to see if there might be some paving underneath this grassy area. And since there is, all I have to do is uncover the rest of the courtyard so I'll have someplace to put the car that won't get muddy when it rains. I want to turn this coach house into a garage. Good idea, no?'

'Great,' said the Commissario. His voice was sharp, his eyes half closed.

'But really!' Fumagalli went on. 'I have to make two turns to get through the entrance on via Lamberti, and even then I have to leave the car under a portico. Much better to come through the park gate and use this coach house.'

Sciancalepre wasn't following Fumagalli's explanation. In one sweeping glance he took in the paving stones, just uncovered, and the powerful hands still holding the pickaxe. He looked up at Fumagalli's face before letting his eyes drop back down to the ground.

Not long afterwards the gardener went to Fumagalli's office early one morning. Closing the door, he told him that he'd recently noticed someone had been clearing the ground in front of the coach house, and against the external wall he'd found a pickaxe normally kept inside with the other tools.

Fumagalli let him go on and Demetrio, with the air of having made a discovery, said he'd suspected some sort of intrusion in the park. For two nights running he'd had a look round at varying times. The first night he'd noticed a man near the coach house. He hadn't had the courage to confront him and had turned back in the direction of the greenhouse. But he saw the shadow come towards him and, frightened, he'd hidden behind the trunk of a magnolia. Peering out from behind it, he noticed that the man went into the greenhouse and moved around inside with an electric lamp he turned on now and again. Demetrio had remained still, waiting, and after a good quarter of an hour he could see the shadow once more, now stretching out towards the coach house. He'd made for the courtyard and left the property by the entrance in the via Lamberti and retreated to his own home. The next night he saw the shadow near the gate, facing outwards as if waiting for someone, but before it moved he thought better of it and stayed away.

'You did well to let me know,' Fumagalli said. 'I've noticed myself that someone's walking around the park at night. But rest assured that sooner or later, one of these nights we'll catch him.'

'I don't want to imply anything,' the gardener added, about to go, 'but I have a suspicion…'

'You think you recognized the shadow?'

'I think so.'

Unwilling to hear another word, Fumagalli tapped his index finger against his nose and shot Demetrio a meaningful look: keep your mouth shut.

He clapped him lightly on the shoulder and dismissed him.

When Sciancalepre was told about the gardener's discovery, he immediately arranged to stake out the grounds on the next moonlit night. There was still a week until the right moment and the new moon; the autumnal sky held only the barest, milky hint of it.

Fumagalli didn't want to put off his work on the garage, so the following day he hired two builders. They prepared the whitewash, began fixing a frame for the rolling shutter and resurfaced the internal walls on the ground floor of the coach house. Having unloaded three carts full of gravel, they set to work taking up the lawn in the courtyard.

The stakeout was set for the night before the full moon, which Sciancalepre thought good enough. It would continue every night until something decisive happened. As a precaution, the Commissario was invited to supper on the night in question so that he wouldn't be seen coming to the house later on.

Silence reigned at table. Although she hadn't been told everything, Signora Emilia seemed very troubled; Sciancalepre tried in vain to make her laugh with a few Neapolitan wisecracks. Teresa, serving that night, was also very anxious. But everyone was hoping for a final conclusion, even a comical one. If things went on as they were, there was some danger of its all turning into a ghost story – featuring some old, long-buried Lamberti, or else the ghostly apparition that had concealed Signora Giulia for the past three years...

So that she should feel able to sleep, Emilia had been told that tonight they would simply try to establish where the nocturnal visitor entered the park. The arrest would take place on another occasion.

By ten, dinner had been over for some time. Teresa had cleared up in the kitchen and gone back home. A little while later Emilia went to her room. She'd been advised to turn out the lights at eleven and not to turn them back on until her husband returned.

At eleven on the dot, Sciancalepre stationed himself on the inside of the gate towards via Lamberti, ears pricked. The moment he heard a faint tap, he silently opened the door to his officer, the young and seriously sturdy Salvatore Pulito, used for operations whenever brute force was called for. Pulito took his place in the hallway with a Coca-Cola, while Sciancalepre and Fumagalli went to the dining-room to drain a bottle of Barolo and smoke a last cigarette before the action.

It was eleven-thirty when they went outside and into the park, Indian file. The moon was already throwing clear shadows. The three of them made for the coach house, avoiding the central pathway and walking along the dividing wall towards the villa Sormani. Pulito stationed himself against one of the gate's pillars in total darkness, in order to block the nightly visitor's retreat; they reckoned he'd end up instead in the beefy arms of the young officer. Sciancalepre and Fumagalli crouched down amongst the low branches of an enormous poplar, ready to leap out at the shadow as soon as it appeared in the courtyard, where it would make as usual for the park's central pathway, and from there to the greenhouse.

After a quarter of an hour they were still cramped under the tree. Fumagalli was itching to move when both of them heard a faint thud, as if someone had leapt over the wall of the villa Sormani, not far from the gate.

'So that's where he comes in,' thought the Commissario. What an ass he was, not to have considered it before!

Time seemed to drag – until the shadow appeared at the edge of the lawned area in front of the coach house. Sciancalepre and Fumagalli both saw him, and instinctively nudged each other in acknowledgement. The black shape appeared in the unlit area and stayed there, as if frightened by so much moonlight falling over the lawn. It wasn't yet midnight; the visitor could consider himself ahead of his usual hour. After a few minutes he started to move, walking over the lawn, in and out of the shadows, straight towards the coach house. He stopped in front of the entrance for a moment, then disappeared inside.

The two men under the tree were impatient. Fumagalli whispered to the Commissario: 'Let's block him inside.'

'No! We must wait until he leaves,' Sciancalepre replied firmly.

The wait continued. Another half hour passed, the shadow neither moving nor making the least bit of noise.

'What do you bet,' Fumagalli whispered again to the Commissario, 'that we've fouled up? It'll be some poor devil, a homeless guy who comes to sleep on the straw in the coach house. And before he falls asleep, he takes a stroll around the park.'

Sciancalepre kept quiet. Without taking his eyes off the entrance to the coach house, he signed that they should go on waiting.

Finally he became impatient and told Fumagalli to cross the glade to the border opposite, right into the moonlight, and then return to their hiding place the same way. Maybe this would encourage the shadow to move.

Content to have something to do, the engineer followed orders. He went out into the clearing and stepped lightly across the lawn, heading for the gate. He stopped for a moment in the shadow, before turning round and beginning the reverse journey, moving just slightly towards the entrance of the coach house so he could hear any sound or sign of life coming from it.

He'd gone about three or four metres beyond the coach house, and was walking back towards the tree where Sciancalepre was waiting, when he caught the sound of a hurried step behind him. Before he could turn round, he saw two flashes from under the poplar and heard two shots. Far away, from the direction of the palazzo, a shriek pierced the air.

Instinctively he threw himself to the ground. He heard running from two or three sides, then the Commissario's voice calling Pulito and, in the sudden silence, one more shot from the revolver.

As soon as Fumagalli could move, the Commissario and Pulito were already helping him up from the ground, afraid that he was wounded. He wanted to know what had happened, but Sciancalepre hurried him towards the villa.

They ran up the stairs and into the house. Fumagalli realized that the scream had come from his wife, who must have been on the balcony and heard the shots. In fact, Emilia was in the hallway, pale and panting. When she saw her husband she felt brighter, but despite all the encouragement to go back to bed, she wanted to hear what had happened.

Sciancalepre was the only one to have seen anything, and he was disinclined to offer much in the way of explanation. He would only say that while he'd been following Fumagalli's return across the lawn, he'd become aware that the shadow had reappeared at the door of the coach house. In a flash, he'd seen it throw itself towards Fumagalli, a powerful club held aloft. He'd immediately shot into the air, arresting the follower's intentions – or he'd certainly have smashed Fumagalli's skull in with the club.

The shadow had fled towards the wall of the villa Sormani, still holding on to his weapon. A few moments later the Commissario had shot blindly in that direction. Then, uncertain whether the heavy blow had hit home, he felt he should help Fumagalli up.

After this brief summary, Sciancalepre was off in a hurry. He took Pulito with him, refusing the offer of a final sip of cognac, and immediately ran to the piazza to look at Esengrini's windows. There, on the second floor, over the office, one light was on in the apartment where the lawyer lived alone.

The Commissario rang the bell, said his name into the entryphone, and immediately heard the click of the automatic entry latch. He left Pulito downstairs while he went up and rang at the door of the flat.

Esengrini came to open the door without making Sciancalepre wait. He was in pyjamas and dressing-gown. Passing through the hallway on his way to the drawing-room, Sciancalepre saw a lamp alight on the night table in the bedroom, and a newspaper on the floor. The lawyer, meanwhile, had sat down in the armchair and welcomed his visitor as if this were a normal visit in the middle of the day.

Sciancalepre was a bit lost for words. 'I've come at this time of night, rather inconsiderately, but to put my mind to rest. Esengrini... it's come to my attention that every now and again, someone creeps into your daughter's villa at night. Since we know it's not thieves, I thought perhaps it might be you? I knew someone who suffered from insomnia and at night, he used to walk about in other people's gardens in order to pass the time – until he took a bullet from a guard. Could it be that you go there from time to time with the key to the gate? Who knows – perhaps to imagine that you're still the owner of the villa?…'

'My dear sir,' the lawyer replied, stretching out in the armchair, 'I understand your suspicions and your concerns, and I realize that you've had to go beyond what was requested in my first charge of abandoning the marital home. Besides me, my wife's disappearance has involved the police, the law, public opinion… Three years have gone by and it's perfectly reasonable to ask why she's never shown any sign of being alive. I myself have thought about everything you have, albeit from another point of view, and with the confidence to exclude myself from a list of probable murderers – if there was one. So I completely understand this visit of yours at one in the morning.'

Sciancalepre seemed relieved. He got up and took his leave. As the lawyer accompanied him to the door, he noticed a huge cherrywood club with a bone handle in the umbrella stand – a solid tool, with which one could kill an ox.

He stopped, took the club from the stand, held it up, tried it out as a walking stick and then brandished it, grasping it near the head. Esengrini watched him calmly.

'Fine club,' Sciancalepre commented.

'I take it whenever I go out at night,' the lawyer explained. 'It was my father's: the stick is cherrywood and the handle's from a deer. A deer's horn!' So saying, he arched his brows and watched the Commissario, his smile forced.

Sciancalepre put the club back in its place, said his good-byes – excusing his intrusion once again – and left.

In the street he began going over the events of the night and wondering how he should put them in the report he'd have to write up. More than a report, it was his duty to file a charge for attempted murder by persons unknown. He almost regretted that he hadn't had the courage to confiscate the lawyer's club, which might constitute a piece of evidence. If he had, however, one could no longer have spoken of 'persons unknown'.

So how could one show that the nocturnal visitor was Esengrini? The legal authorities would in any case make this conclusion. But with what proof?

SIX

Sciancalepre had more or less completed his report by around eleven the next morning and was just polishing it off with the phrase, 'This record will be followed by further investigations, still ongoing, to establish the identification of the suspect, etc., etc…' when the door to his office swung open and Fumagalli literally ran into his desk. Pale as death, he gasped out the astonishing words to Sciancalepre's face: 'Signora Giulia… she's been found! Found! There's no doubt that it's her. Even her suitcases are there.'

It was five minutes before he'd caught his breath enough to continue.

'This morning,' he said, 'the builders went into the grounds as usual to continue their work on the garage. I came down late because I hadn't been able to get to sleep until dawn, and I went to see last night's scene of the crime. I picked up the three bullets you'd fired from off the ground, then went to look at the wall of the villa Sormani where our secret guest entered.

'I noticed that around six or seven metres from the gate there's an iron stirrup fixed at the height of one metre on the boundary wall. I climbed up the wall and saw that the ground on the Sormani side of the park is at least one metre higher than it is in our part of the park. It would be easy, even for an old person, to cross over from the villa Sormani into ours using the protruding iron stirrup to jump over the wall, and then return the same way.'

'But Signora Giulia?!' The Commissario was at the very limit of his patience.

Fumagalli went on. 'While I was trying to scale the wall, one of my builders called me. I went over to the clearing in front of the coach house and saw that they'd finished uncovering the paving stones. The builder took me to a square manhole they'd opened by removing a large stone fitted with a ring. Demetrio, who was there, said it was a cistern for collecting rainwater. The cistern and its manhole had been hidden for at least thirty years by the grass that had grown over the old courtyard.

'Looking down into the cistern, you could clearly see a large suitcase. The builders told me that as soon as they'd removed the manhole, an intense smell of fungus and mulch came out of it. Nearer the opening, there was an odour almost like a damp forest floor. I sent someone to fetch an electric lamp and I went down into the cistern where there were five centimetres of water. A little further on, a human form appeared under the beam of light. I saw two feet in women's shoes, two thin shin-bones… and, as I shone the light along the body… the face of Signora Giulia, easily recognizable. It didn't seem possible that I could make her out so well when she'd been in that grave for three years. They had to pull me out of the cistern because my own legs wouldn't hold me up. I had them shut it up again immediately and I ran right here.'

They remained silent for a few minutes. Sciancalepre was thinking.

The report stood in the typewriter, wanting only a few concluding lines. Now he knew how he should complete them.

Speaking more to himself than to Fumagalli, he reconstructed the facts: 'The lawyer Esengrini, having discovered his wife's affair with Barsanti, wrote him the famous letter in order to persuade him to get out of the area. When Thursday came along, realizing that his wife was preparing to leave for Milan and that the situation was ongoing, he came back from court and confronted his wife, telling her everything he suspected. I can almost hear him: "You go to Milan, you run to Emilia's school, then you take a taxi to viale Premuda to such and such a number where Luciano's waiting for you..."

'I can see it all. Accusations, counter-accusations, then the sudden fury, maybe after her heartless confession. His hands on her neck... he loses his mind for a moment... and seconds later her limp body falls to the ground. He's momentarily terrified, he's confused – and then he comes to, with the lucid rationality of a legal man, an expert in crime and evidence.

'Through the cellar – so as not to cross the internal courtyard – and into the park, dragging the cadaver behind him – or rather, carrying it in his arms... I've thought about this journey so often, always wondering where it ended up. And lately I've walked the park so many times, looking for a grave – I've even brought a trained dog along. But Signora Giulia was lying underneath a stone, with its edges sunk into the ground and grass clumps carefully rearranged over it all. Who could have dreamt of this cistern!

'So the lawyer went out through the cellar into the park, reached the coach house, removed the clumps of grass, opened the manhole, which he knew about, and threw the corpse into the void. Then he went back to the house and faked her escape. He packed her bags with some linens and a few clothes, filling

69

the overnight case with jewellery and other small items. One of the cases was too large and wouldn't go through the manhole. So he took a smaller one, leaving the other in his wife's room. After having thrown the suitcases into the cistern he closed it up again, stuck the grass clumps around it in the right places and went back into the house.

'All of it had to have happened between midday and one, after Teresa had gone home. And here the account tallies, because Teresa said that she was in the lawyer's house that morning to clean as usual, just as always. But Signora Giulia sent her back, telling her to return at eleven. At eleven, when she returned, she hurried to finish in half an hour since she didn't have to prepare lunch on Thursdays: Signora Giulia, who was leaving by the two o'clock train, set the table herself and at twenty to two went off, leaving everything in a mess.

'Teresa came back at two, cleared the table, washed up and worked with the other maid who always came at around two since Signora Giulia liked to be alone in the house in the morning. All went perfectly: between midday and one. At two-thirty he was with me, reporting the drama. He'd been waiting from one-thirty: time to get himself together. He told me he hadn't even eaten. I'm sure he hadn't!' And with that, Sciancalepre got up.

'Let's go there,' he said. 'We'll stop first to pick up a doctor, the magistrate and a registrar, and we'll identify the body. The rest will take care of itself.'

Just in case, he sent a sergeant and officer Pulito to watch the lawyer's office and house, with orders not to lose sight of him if he left the house and to stop him if he got into a car. Then he set off for the magistrates' court with Fumagalli.

The magistrate, having been filled in, in turn phoned the public prosecutor's office and asked for advice. He was told to go ahead and apprehend Esengrini as soon as the body had been identified.

Just as the group was leaving the magistrates' court to head for the villa, Esengrini came through the door, Sciancalepre's two men some distance behind him. He calmly went to look at the papers on a case set for the next day. It wasn't a dramatic encounter. Fumagalli, who wasn't speaking to his father-in-law, had gone on ahead.

'Where are you off to? Some crime scene?'

The magistrate cut him off. 'Sir, you're coming too. We're going to your daughter's villa to look into something that concerns you.'

The lawyer looked at his son-in-law, who'd stopped with his back to the group. He looked at the Commissario, who'd lowered his head. He put a hand on his shoulder. 'Have you found something?' he asked in a hushed voice.

'Yes,' the Commissario answered, 'something crucial.'

Meanwhile, the sergeant and Pulito had approached, and Esengrini realized that he'd been followed from his office door. Without another word, he set out with the group beside the Commissario. No one, seeing them go by, could have imagined what was going on.

There was hardly anyone about. It was a Thursday. Another of Signora Giulia's Thursdays.

When they arrived at the entrance in via Lamberti, Esengrini was let in second, after the magistrate. Emilia was in the house but she didn't know anything was up; no one had told her yet about the find. The squad went down the flight of stairs and into the park as far as the coach house. They arrived in the clearing, where Demetrio and the two builders were standing at some distance from the closed-up manhole, waiting.

The magistrate asked for it to be opened. More lamps were brought and the Commissario produced a torch from under his overcoat and gave it to Pulito, ordering him to climb into the well and bring out the two suitcases.

It was a long and difficult operation. Esengrini stood by stiffly, looking down into the opening. He indicated recognition of the suitcases with a nod. The suitcases were placed side by side and opened. One was stuffed with crumpled linens and slimy, wet clothing. The overnight case contained just two small purses: one was empty and in the other there was a lipstick, a rusted compact, a tissue, some keys, a pair of gloves and a wallet which was opened in order to take out the bit of cash that was in it: six thousand lire in total. There were also a few cards in it, a photo of Emilia, an identity card, a little notebook. Everything was soaked with water and mud, and coated in coffee-coloured mould.

After a thorough examination of the suitcases, the Commissario entered the cistern. The magistrate lay down on some newspapers spread over the ground around the opening and put his head into the void. He could see a dark form illuminated by the torch, apparently floating on a veil of black water.

After an hour's work the body was brought up and laid out on the ground with the help of the two builders. They had to use a canvas, because the limbs were falling off.

Fumagalli had gone up to the house to stop his wife – who might have become suspicious or been told something by

Teresa – from coming into the park and being confronted by the scene. He'd also telephoned a photographer at the magistrate's request, and shortly afterwards there were photos of everything, especially the cadaver.

There was no doubt about its identity. Esengrini was the first to say: 'It's her.'

Her face, once so pale, had turned honey-coloured and transparent. Her undamaged hair spread over the ground, and from between the trees a ray of sun threw over it a warm reflection, so that it might almost have been confused with the dry, crumpled leaves spread across the lawn.

Her clothes were faded and practically moulded to her body, like those of a statue. The graceful, lively figure of Signora Giulia was no longer recognizable in that form. Stretched out along the ground, she looked like a dressed-up skeleton. A pool of putrefaction, which the paving stones couldn't soak up, slowly formed around her. Her hair alone seemed immune to transformation; it was loose in a way no one there had ever seen apart from her husband. Her head seemed like that of a young girl, and except for the empty eye sockets strongly recalled her daughter's face around the cheekbones and forehead. When they moved her, a thick, dark liquid flowed out of the sockets. Her golden wedding band was removed from her ring finger. Inside the circle, the date of her wedding was still legible.

The corpse was taken to the morgue for an autopsy, and in order to get it out, the gate on the country road was opened. The old key hanging on the nail in the coach house still worked. The van arrived, and Signora Giulia made her last journey.

The magistrate, the registrar, the Commissario and Pulito remained, along with Esengrini and the two officers. There wasn't much joking in the conversation that followed.

'Esengrini,' said the magistrate, 'I've telephoned the court and informed them fully. They suggest a provisional arrest. I don't know what to say to you: you'll defend yourself. Sciancalepre will accompany you to the cells. Let's go out by the gate – that way we'll avoid onlookers.'

Sciancalepre felt no need to speak. He stood beside the lawyer, head bowed. Then, leaving the magistrate at the end of the pathway, he went the short distance to the cells with his prisoner. The guard let them through, as on so many other occasions, thinking that they needed to speak to someone inside.

Instead, his mouth agape, he had to welcome the lawyer himself amongst his guests.

His orders carried out, Sciancalepre went straight home. For the first time in his life, he wasn't thinking about his spaghetti at that hour. His head whirled with a jumble of thoughts and problems. The jewellery hadn't been found, either in the suitcases or at the bottom of the cistern, even though it had been thoroughly searched.

In the records, there was an inventory of the jewellery Signora Giulia had taken with her. Esengrini himself had reconstructed the list: four diamond rings, three pairs of earrings, a strand of pearls, a diamond necklace, two pins set with precious stones, a watch and two bracelets also set with diamonds.

Sciancalepre could recall the jewellery by heart. He'd seen it who knows how many times on the poor woman. Where had all that stuff gone? He thought about making a detailed search of the lawyer's house and office and felt some hope. And suddenly it occurred to him that neither he nor the magistrate had charged Esengrini with the crime of homicide; and that Esengrini hadn't made the slightest admission of being the perpetrator of the crime. He'd attended the identification of the corpse as an interested bystander, but had never shown any sign of confusion.

At table he gave his wife the news. The plate she'd been holding fell to the floor.

'How was Signora Giulia?' she asked.

'Falling apart, poor thing – it was indescribable! Those empty sockets… Only her hair was untouched. At least there was no smell. She was all shrivelled up…'

For the time being, Esengrini's arrest was a simple matter of police custody. But that afternoon Sciancalepre decided to complete his report with an explicit charge for the murder of Giulia Zaccagni-Lamberti and of the attempted murder of Carlo Fumagalli. He went to the public prosecutor's office to deliver his report in person, stopped by police headquarters to accept the chief's congratulations and then went back home.

Two days later the public prosecutor, having notified Esengrini of the two charges against him and the warrant for his arrest, went to M—— for the questioning. At the old district prison of M——, built one hundred years before by the Austrians, Esengrini was brought into the little room reserved for judges and lawyers – without tie, shoelaces or belt. And yet his natural distinction was in no way diminished. On the contrary, an air of being both offended and annoyed heightened the pitch of his words and the looks he gave.

The magistrate prepared to hear a full confession. But first he waited for the court clerk to take down all the accused's personal details as required by the State. The official was about to write 'married with issue' when Esengrini firmly corrected him. 'Widower', he said, his arched brows underscoring the word.

When the court clerk had finished writing the usual phrase, 'The accused, charged with crimes as specified in the warrant for arrest, responds', the prosecutor said courteously: 'You dictate it, Esengrini.'

Esengrini agreed with a nod and began to dictate.

'I deny having committed the first crime charged against me at A, of having somehow taken part, or of having caused others to commit it. I deny having committed the crime listed in the second charge at B.'

He then asked the clerk for a pen to sign with.

'Just a minute!' the magistrate exclaimed. 'What do you mean, you deny it?'

'I deny it.'

'Then I have some questions to put to you.'

'Go ahead.'

'How do you explain the fact that the cadaver's been in your villa for three years?'

'I'm not explaining anything,' the detainee concluded. 'For the time being it's not up to me to explain. It's up to you to demonstrate that I killed my wife and that it was my shadow armed with the club. If I have to, I will appeal during the course of the inquiry. It's only now that I've learnt that there was an attempted murder in the park the other night. Now I understand why Sciancalepre arrived at my house at one in the morning with such a face. I must reflect, sir; I've got to collect my thoughts. For the moment I can tell you only that I am innocent.'

In truth, the prosecution still lacked evidence. Sciancalepre's reconstruction was based on nothing but supposition – it was reasonably logical, but that wasn't proof. The only fruit of the painstaking search of the lawyer's home and office for the jewellery was the confiscated club. Two safe-deposit boxes at the bank had been inspected with similar results: nothing.

Sciancalepre worked on an hour-by-hour reconstruction of the morning of the crime, and Esengrini was questioned for a second time. He explained that he had come back to the house at noon and found it in the same state as that in which the Commissario had found it two hours later. Teresa confirmed that she had been sent away from the house at nine by Signora Giulia; that she'd come back at eleven and had heard the signora in her room. She'd gone away for sure at eleven-thirty and returned only at two, when the signora was no longer there. But the door had been closed.

SEVEN

While the investigators scoured Rome for Luciano Barsanti, Esengrini put in a request for his own confrontation with Barsanti. The appeal was granted, and a few days after their face-to-face, he was able to set down a few facts:

1. that Barsanti had received the famous letter exactly four days before the crime;
2. that Barsanti did not remember having shredded or destroyed it, but in any case he hadn't saved it and couldn't put his hand on it;
3. that Barsanti had sold his furniture from the flat on viale Premuda to a shopkeeper in via Fiori Chiari, four or five days after receiving the letter;
4. that he'd moved to Rome the next day;
5. that in one of his first letters to Signora Giulia he had told her about having at last found an apartment at viale Premuda, n. XY;
6. that he had signed some of his letters with his Christian name, and others with both Christian name and surname.

After the meeting Esengrini went back to his cell, asked for paper, pen and ink, and made another appeal to the authorities. He requested an inspection of his office and a search for the Molinari file: S.I.R.C.E. In the folder a sealed yellow envelope would be found with 'Molinari Accounts: supporting documentation' written on it. The envelope was to be opened by the investigators, who would find in it conclusive proof in the form of the famous letter received by Barsanti.

The magistrate couldn't understand where Esengrini was going with this or how the letter had come into his possession. He had the feeling that he was playing a game of chess with the ablest of adversaries, to whose moves he had to submit from the moment he failed to prevent them.

He went to the lawyer's office, found the file and the large yellow envelope inside it, and opened it seated at Esengrini's desk. Inside, he discovered two letters in their envelopes, one of them typewritten on the Esengrini office letterhead with the old address in via Lamberti and addressed to Luciano Barsanti, viale Premuda, n. XY. He read:

M——, 15 May 1955.

Dear Sir,

I am aware of your arrangement with my wife Giulia. I have no intention of causing a scandal and I advise you to put an end to the situation. Should you fail to do so I will pursue the matter with the utmost rigour. I rely on your good sense and alert you to the fact that I am prepared to take action that would see you in jail. Don't mention this letter to my wife: it would only be perpetuating the betrayal.

It was signed by Esengrini.

The magistrate was stymied. How could the letter have come into Esengrini's hands? He found the explanation in the other letter. It was in an envelope with the letterhead of another lawyer, Attilio Panelli of Milan, via Marsiglia, n. XX, and was worded precisely as follows:

Milan, 20 May 1957.

Dear Colleague,

The enclosed letter with your address on it was found in the drawer of one of the items of furniture in the forced sale of effects during the course of proceedings against one Antonio Nanni and the sale of effects previously seized from said Nanni, trading in used furniture from the warehouse in via Fiori Chiari, n. XX. As the letter concerns neither the accused nor my client, I thought it best to return it to you, thereby preventing matters relating to your private life from coming to the attention of strangers.

Cordially,

Attilio Panelli

So, the magistrate reasoned, Barsanti had forgotten the letter at the back of a drawer. The furniture, sold by the rag-and-bone man of via Fiori Chiari, had ended up at auction and the letter, falling into the hands of the lawyer Panelli had, with the delicacy of a colleague, been returned to sender.

But of what interest was it to Esengrini to produce it now? Hadn't he always denied having written it? The letter appeared to have been sent from M——on a Saturday, and to have arrived in Milan on the following Monday. Three days later, on Thursday, Signora Giulia had disappeared. Barsanti's statement regarding his encounter with the lawyer corresponded with the truth.

An idea began to take shape in the magistrate's mind: that Esengrini was tightening the grip around Barsanti. At any rate, he'd set things up for an arrest.

While the young man, arrested in Rome, was travelling under escort towards the prison in M——, Esengrini, informed of the discovery of the yellow envelope, made another surprising request. It was his method when defending and the public prosecutor had seen it in action at other times. Begrudgingly, he had to pass the proceedings to the examining judge, presenting the case as rather complex and, as such, requesting a formal investigation.

The new petition to the examining judge demanded the seizure of Esengrini's diary for 1955, saved in the office archives. The judge looked at the page for the Saturday when the letter to Barsanti was sent. There he found the following annotations:

— meeting with the lawyer Berrini on the Bassetti file
— meeting with Egidio Rossinelli and family on the suit against Scardìa
— appointment with the surveyor Chiodetti
— request for provisional freedom: Alfredo Marchionato (N 468/62)

Envisioning further requests from Esengrini, and curious to see him, the examining judge went to visit him in prison.

'Sir,' he heard Esengrini say, 'perhaps you understand where I'm going with this; I therefore advise the utmost secrecy. Go ahead looking into things on your own. But we're at a crucial point: just one word is all that's needed to destroy the definitive proof. Don't even speak with a colleague; don't let a single soul look at the proceedings. My liberty is at stake. The guilty man is nearby, with eyes and ears open. We need to convince him that by this point, I'm done for…

'I've been studying the documents I'm putting in the file for you for years and they have revealed the truth to me. Looking through them, I've identified the killer, reconstructed his actions and finally, five months ago, I discovered the corpse of my wife in the cistern. (This revelation is just for you.) When I had to leave the house where I'd spent twenty-one years with my wife, I felt I was in danger, but I defied that danger. I had, and I have, a careful adversary, as able as I but more determined, capable of killing again to save himself. An adversary who's aware of my painstaking work to reconstruct the truth.'

'But who is he?' asked the judge. 'It's time to talk, Esengrini. You don't trust the law!'

'Sir, if I told you that I trusted the law I'd be lying. I trust you, I trust in your intelligence, your utter rectitude, and that of all magistrates. But I don't trust the law. Justice is a machine with neither heart nor intelligence: it acts as instructed. And the instruction is determined by the evidence. We must feed it firm evidence, documents, reliable witness statements. Then it will strike accurately. Heaven help us if we feed it with opinions! Or worse, if we stuff it with incomplete or vague evidence…'

'So then, what's the next move?'

'I would ask you to seal off my office, including the internal space and the windows, and put an officer there to sleep nights. Then I'd ask you to get hold of the file containing the proceedings against Alfredo Marchionato: drawer 468/62 – it's archived in the magistrates' court. It concerns an action for libel, which we won. I was the defender. In the trial there's a request from

83

me for provisional liberty. I drew it up that Saturday, as you saw in my diary.'

The judge looked into the Marchionato trial and found the request for provisional liberty, typewritten and signed by the lawyer. He added everything to the records.

Meanwhile the details of the investigation were coming in to him. The lawyer Panelli confirmed having found the letter in the drawer of the furniture at auction. The same bailiff remembered the details.

The results of the autopsy also came through. The forensic pathologist had immediately stated that a three-year-old cadaver would reveal nothing, and in fact his report left the cause of death as undetermined. It could have been strangulation or drowning. The internal cavities were full of sand, mould and small algae that had passed through the oral cavity during the body's submersion, when rainfall had raised the level of the water in the cistern. There were no broken bones in the cervical region. The carotid cartilage had been destroyed by decomposition and didn't provide any evidence. Signs of breakage could only have been preserved in the event of a natural mummification. But the effects of the water and the airless environment had subjected the body of Signora Giulia to a type of partial saponification. The facial planes were partially preserved, and thanks to their having become waxy it had been possible to identify the dead woman's face as soon as she was discovered, an identification confirmed by the wedding ring. The cause of death had to be considered violent. Whoever had hidden that body – dead or alive – down in the cistern was the killer or his accomplice.

While the magistrate gathered the results, Sciancalepre came forward with some news. The grocer Lucchini had spontaneously presented himself to the Commissario in order to state that he'd met Esengrini fifteen days before his arrest in via Lamberti, at one-thirty in the morning in the neighbourhood of the palazzo Zaccagni-Lamberti. The grocer, returning home from his shop after having finished an inventory of his goods, bumped into the lawyer. The fact made an impression on him since at M—— everyone knew that relations between the lawyer and his daughter were not good. So when he heard about the arrest and the charge, he felt it his duty to come in. He didn't mention that he was doing it gladly, since four years before Esengrini had upheld the plaintiff against him in a trial for commercial fraud and he'd been convicted. Apart from these proceedings, the incident could have some bearing on the murder of Signora Giulia; or rather, the wife-killing, as the papers called it, so the grocer had done his duty.

The judge added Lucchini's deposition to the record and took the opportunity to speak to Esengrini about other details. Esengrini admitted without hesitation having met the grocer that night; and so as not to tantalize him too much confided another piece of the truth to him.

'At this stage, I must tell you, sir, that my means of entry to the park wasn't the gate of the palazzo Zaccagni-Lamberti, but the one adjacent to the palazzo Sormani, to which I'd obtained the key. From the courtyard of the palazzo Sormani, I went through to the park, then climbed over the wall towards the back. I went in after midnight, when everyone in the palazzo was in bed. No one could see me go in. There's a bend in the road there, and before entering I'd stand listening in order to be certain that there were no night-owls around. However, there *was* someone who saw me…'

'Lucchini,' the judge offered timidly.

'Lucchini,' the lawyer confirmed, 'and not only Lucchini. But this is part of another revelation that I'll make in a few days. Now I'd ask you to question all the people who came to my office that Saturday morning: the lawyer Berrini, Signor Egidio Rossinelli, his wife and sister-in-law, and the surveyor Chiodetti. That morning in my office must be reconstructed.'

It was no simple feat. The lawyer, Berrini, didn't remember anything any more, but he didn't rule it out: he had discussed the Bassetti file with Esengrini. He went to see his colleague frequently as their offices were so close together, and he couldn't be precise.

The Rossinelli were more precise. In their entire lives they had fought only the one lawsuit, against some neighbours – the Scardìas, southerners – for damage and unlawful entry. A backyard squabble. That morning – and the date was confirmed by the lodging of the complaint – they'd gone to Esengrini's office to lay out the facts and request him to act on their behalf. It wasn't just Egidio Rossinelli; his wife and sister-in-law also remembered having been there for nearly an hour and having helped draft the complaint, which Esengrini dictated to the typist.

Egidio recalled that as he was going into the office, Berrini was coming out of it. One of those ideal witnesses who end up remembering too much, he recalled that Demetrio was in the office as well – indeed that it had been Demetrio who'd advised him to lodge the suit the day before. He then found in the recesses of his prodigious memory that there had also been a very elegant man in the office that Saturday morning – something no one else remembered.

The surveyor Chiodetti remembered having provided Esengrini with an estimate for a property that day, and he found the evidence in his diary. Yet another one with a good memory, he managed to recall that the lawyer had been out of his office; he'd had to wait for him.

It wasn't difficult for the intelligent magistrate to finalize the deposition by doing a little sleuthing: Esengrini had presented the Rossinelli suit in person in court that Saturday. So the lawyer had drafted the lawsuit, gone with his clients to court to present it and returned to his office, where he'd found Chiodetti waiting for him.

With these final witness examinations and his files on the investigation, the magistrate went to the prison in M—— to wring the final revelations from Esengrini.

Esengrini was satisfied and said to him in a very friendly manner: 'I told you I have no faith in the law; in abstract justice, that is. And you – without taking offence, you had faith in me, the accused. If only it were always like this!'

The magistrate accepted the compliment. But then he sat down and told Esengrini it was time to come clean.

'So it is,' Esengrini accepted. 'I'll tell you everything, apart from the name of the killer. Prepare to have a bit more patience and another measure of faith in the accused. You should know that even before our diligent Sciancalepre, I was convinced my wife couldn't have fled, but had been killed. I was certain of it after Sciancalepre's famous trip to Rome, when he learnt about the letter Barsanti had received, which I was sure I'd never written.

'It was the killer who wrote that letter. But only I could think so; as far as everyone else was concerned, the letter was written by me. So I would have had to be aware of the relationship between my wife and Barsanti, and hence the jealousy, the threats, the midday skirmish with my wife that Thursday, the murder, the faked escape. I've asked myself a thousand times why you didn't arrest me! The logical proof was nearly there… I wanted to deny having written the letter! I repeat: I wondered how you could close the file.'

'Esengrini, it was not only the letter that was missing, but also the body.'

'You're right; they were both missing. And they were the first things I looked for. The body couldn't be far away. The murder took place in the house and the spot most suited for hiding the body was in the grounds. When I found out that the grounds had been searched with a dog (Demetrio told me), I shuddered. She wasn't buried in the grounds, thank goodness. And if she had been, I can tell you that I would have changed the spot if I'd been able, since it would have spelt my death sentence: I didn't yet have the proof to hand that you now have in the file!'

'But what proof!' exclaimed the judge.

'What's there now. All of it, apart from one thing: I don't know where her jewellery is. About six months ago, I found a letter in the post from Panelli, the lawyer from Milan. A mysterious hand was helping me. I'm not a believer, still less am I superstitious, but that discovery, so unexpected, seemed like a sign from the heavens. I came to believe that that poor little thing wanted justice, and had had no peace, knowing I was suspected of her death.

'You can't imagine what these past three years have been like for me! My daughter's hatred – first she gets engaged and then married to her mother's ex-suitor – the looks from my colleagues and clients, the magistrate's behaviour… Everyone was convinced that I was a cunning murderer.

'When I opened the letter, I couldn't believe my eyes. There was the phantom document! The letterhead was mine, the signature could have been mine. I began to fear actually having been my wife's killer, of having acted unconsciously, by doubling, like vampires. During that period I'd been skimming a book called *I Believe in Vampires*, which spoke of the dead who return to the world without a conscience and suck the blood of the living in an attempt to regain the lives they've lost. I thought I was one of them. I believed, too, in vampires, in Doctor Jekyll, in the doubling of Dorian Gray – that character in the famous novel by Oscar Wilde.

'I'd killed my wife myself, without knowing it, and buried her in the grounds or in the cellar. I remembered that cellar, with its exit near the greenhouse under the embankment the palazzo Zaccagni-Lamberti is built on. For three years, I'd never thought once about it. I went all over it for several days. I shifted the paving, even knocked on the walls. Nothing. But by dint of searching under a pile of smashed demijohns and wooden tables, I found a cloth button from a dress my wife had been wearing in the last days I saw her – it's missing from her wardrobe – perhaps the same one she put on the morning of her death. It's for that reason I requested that the cadaver's clothes be produced as evidence.'

'Will we find a button missing?' asked the judge.

'That button was actually another thing against me,' the

89

lawyer continued. 'However, I had to save it because it would become part of the jigsaw I was constructing. I put it back where I'd found it; that was the best hiding place. We'll go together to retrieve it when the moment's right. But it's a trifling thing, and it doesn't shift the blame from me to anyone else. They'll only move the jewellery definitely when they find it. That is, *if* they find it. The killer's ingenious, and he's playing a difficult game with me. The jewellery is a crucial tool in his hands. If it could be hidden in my office or my house, I'd be finished. That's why I asked for my office to be guarded by a policeman after the search. I feared – and I still fear – that the killer, seeing that the investigation is not winding up, or suspecting it's going to broaden out to include to him, will opt to sacrifice the jewellery, and go to hide it in my office, where a thorough search will uncover it.

'But let's move on. When I found the button I began to think that the body could have been hidden during the day and then brought outside, who knows where. It wouldn't have been easy, but it would have been possible. I felt I was close, incredibly close to solving the case! I walked around the grounds continually during the day while my daughter was at university in Milan. I examined every dirt clod. Now and again I took a pickaxe and dug somewhere, covering it up later.

'One day, dead tired after digging along the wall near the villa Sormani, I started back to the coach house with the axe. I was dragging the thing on the ground, I was so exhausted. All at once it slipped from my grasp. It had got stuck in a hook on the lawn in front of the coach house, as if a hand had seized it. When I went to fetch it, I noticed that in dragging it I'd unearthed a large iron ring.

'I tried to tug it up; it was stuck. I pulled up several handfuls of grass, and a manhole cover appeared. I struggled to lift it. It was embedded in the ground, with the edges sunk into the earth. Hardly had I moved it when a gust of damp air hit me. I'd discovered my wife's grave.

'I carefully closed it up again, sinking the ring into the earth and covering it up with grass. Now I knew everything. But I was certain that the jewellery wouldn't be found in the suitcases. It was booty worth at least thirty million lire, and the killer couldn't have thrown that away.

'Meanwhile, events moved swiftly forward. My daughter was about to reach the age of majority. She got married without a word to me. On the same day, Sciancalepre came to tell me that I had to leave the villa; my daughter was now the owner. I left. The only thing I cared about was still being able to enter the grounds, and I made sure of this. Since I'm the administrator for the Sormani property, I have the keys of the door opening onto via Lamberti. That's how I began my life as the night shadow. A shadow with little hope, since the jewellery could hardly have been in the grounds. The killer had hidden it very well, and had I accused him – with what proof? – he could easily have pointed the finger back at me.'

At this point Esengrini suddenly became very tired. His head fell to his breast and he closed his eyes. 'Leave me,' he said to the judge. 'Come back tomorrow. I've had heart trouble for a little while now...'

The magistrate left. The next day he was at M——first thing in the morning. He found the prisoner in fine condition and he prepared to listen to the end of the story, which had kept him awake all night.

But Esengrini had another request to put forward. He asked the judge to carry out an experiment: to take Marchionato's petition for provisional liberty and the letter said to be from Esengrini to Barsanti and put the two sheets on top of one another, place them against a window and compare the two signatures.

The judge, who had the file with him, carried out the experiment against the window of the little room. The two signatures fit together perfectly. Only the dots of the two 'i's didn't fit. 'This signature was traced using a transparency!' he exclaimed, looking at the letter.

'Of course. And it's the key to the mystery. Now you see why I told you the killer had written the letter. That's the signature of the killer! And it was signed that Saturday!'

'But where are you leading me, Esengrini?' cried the judge. 'Talk! Out with the name! My patience is limited. I've done everything you've asked me to do. I'm not going any further in the dark.'

'I can't yet tell you the name. First I must find the jewellery. And I want to find it without leaving prison. Help me out a bit longer. Not even the attorney general of the court of assizes can uphold the charge without the jewellery.'

'Esengrini,' said the investigating judge, 'after this experiment with the two signatures, which I'm going to submit for an expert opinion even though there's no need for it, you need only come out with his name and I'll order your release.'

'Not on your life! I'm going to stay inside until they find the jewellery. I'm going out when "he" comes in. If "he" knew I was out, he'd know his time was up and he might make some unpredictable move.'

EIGHT

The judge went off to await further requests from Esengrini.

In the meantime, Sciancalepre hadn't been sitting on his thumbs. By this time the case had been referred to the investigating judge, but no one was stopping Sciancalepre collecting more information.

He remembered having overlooked something. Given that Teresa Foletti had received a letter from Barsanti after Signora Giulia's disappearance, then Barsanti could have received some of her letters in viale Premuda after he'd left for Rome. In which case the doorkeeper, not knowing Barsanti's new address, should have kept the correspondence. Sciancalepre therefore decided to return to viale Premuda, in spite of the three-year gap.

Meanwhile, he wanted to look again into the nocturnal visitor's route of entry into the property. He went to the villa, climbed over the wall with the aid of the iron stirrup, and dropped into the Sormani property. Just there, the ground level was higher than it was in the Zaccagni-Lamberti property, something Fumagalli had already pointed out.

But how did the visitor get into the Sormani property? Sciancalepre asked himself. The villa Sormani also had iron railings on the side facing the country and on the via Lamberti side it was closed off by the palazzo. For anyone not coming from inside the Sormani house, it had to amount to one and the same: climbing over one set of railings or the other. So why the Sormani gate and not directly from the Zaccagni-Lamberti side? It was a little conundrum to add to all the others. And as if that were not enough, Sciancalepre encountered yet another: walking round the Sormani grounds, he found the handle of a new pickaxe under the dry leaves that slid underfoot; a veritable club, with squared edges on the part that entered the iron head. He picked it up, scaled the wall once more and went to the coach house where the workmen were still busy. He asked them if they were missing the handle of one of their pickaxes.

Several days before, they responded – in fact, the day that the cadaver had come to light – they'd discovered that a new axe, one they'd brought along with the other tools, was missing its wooden handle. They showed it to Sciancalepre and he matched it with the handle he'd found under the leaves, noting its perfect fit with the iron part. Was this handle, then, the club he had seen the shadow figure holding over Fumagalli's head? He confiscated the axe and took down the builders' names.

Serious doubts began to creep into Sciancalepre's mind. The same wearisome delays in the investigation and certain inquiries about which he'd heard rumours gave him a hunch that Signora Giulia's killing could have an entirely different explanation from the one he'd settled on.

Like Hamlet, he kept asking himself, *The axe or the club? A club with a handle of horn – or the wooden handle of an axe? And why did Esengrini go through the Sormani grounds?* He thought about Domenico Sormani, unmarried brother of the head of the family, a gambler and ladies' man known for his love affairs. For half an hour, he tried to reconstruct a secret dalliance between

Sormani and poor Signora Giulia. But then he remembered that for the whole of the year concerned, Domenico Sormani had been in South America, where his brother had a business. He abandoned that line of thinking and decided to take up the thread on the viale Premuda once more.

The following day he was in Milan. He recognized the same doorkeeper, still there. He identified himself and tried to get her to recall his visit of three years ago.

'It seems to me,' she said coldly, 'that three years ago someone did come to look for the tenant on the top floor, that young man who was always seeing women.'

'That was me,' Sciancalepre pressed on, 'with some officers from the police station. But tell me, that tenant who went to Rome without leaving his address, did he receive any more post here?'

'I have a stack of letters for tenants who've left and have never come back to claim correspondence. Sometimes it arrives a few years after they've gone,' the doorkeeper said. 'Let's see…'

She went down to the lower ground floor, where she had a living-room, and returned with a packet of letters. She let Sciancalepre go through them and to his astonishment there appeared, among the last three, an envelope which read:

Signor Luciano Barsanti

There, on a yellowed envelope covered with fingerprints, was Signora Giulia's handwriting, somewhat faded with time.

Sciancalepre sat down and recorded the discovery, asking the doorkeeper to sign the report. He hurried to M—— and rushed like lightning through his office in order to grab the packet containing the axe and its handle. He gave it to officer Pulito to carry, and the two of them headed to the chief's office.

The letter burned in his pocket. He'd thought it prudent, at this stage in the inquiry, not to open it, and to place everything in the hands of the investigating judge.

'Let's open it together,' said the judge, after hearing the results of the Commissario's latest efforts.

The letter was dated the Thursday of Signora Giulia's disappearance and said:

> *My dear Luciano,*
>
> *Perhaps today I'll wait in vain. Just when you're leaving, things are getting more complicated. From the beginning of our affair, someone has known about it. I never said anything to you because I knew that any kind of difficulty bothered you. But maybe today, what I've always feared will come true. Do I wait for everything to be discovered? Face the consequences? If my husband throws me out, it will actually be liberating. Don't be afraid of anything. I'll never give him your name, and no one will ever know how happy I was in your arms. And if some day I'm free and feel sure that I won't drag you down, I'll come and find you… I'll go and see your sister in Tuscany, and she'll tell me where you are. It's the only dream I have left.*
>
> *Your Giulia*

'Poor woman!' murmured Sciancalepre.

The judge, however, exclaimed, 'Fantastic! Wonderful! Now I'm sure Esengrini is innocent.' And turning to Sciancalepre: 'Let's go get the killer.'

'But what killer?' asked Sciancalepre.

'Oh, that's right. You're not *au fait* with Esengrini's declaration and petition. Here – take this file and read the whole thing while I go and hear a couple of witnesses. Then we'll drive to M—— and on the way you'll tell me the killer's name. I think we'll be in agreement.'

Sciancalepre wouldn't even have read the will of an American uncle with such delight.

When he found the famous apocryphal letter from Esengrini to Barsanti and repeated the experiment with the overlay at the window, his face lit up. But confronted with the signed notes in the lawyer's diary, his thoughts once again became muddled. He turned his mind back, and tried to imagine how and when Signora Giulia could have written the letter to Barsanti that Thursday. Evidently at around nine that morning, when she'd sent Teresa Foletti back home. But who had 'known about it'? Surely whoever had traced the signature of Esengrini. And if they'd traced it from the document containing the request for Marchionato's provisional liberty, the operation must have taken place in Esengrini's office in his absence. But when? The previous Saturday. And that explained why Esengrini had put forward the request for the sequestration of his office. That Saturday morning, the request for Marchionato's provisional liberty had lain on Esengrini's table, typed up and already signed. The lawyer Berrini had already been in Esengrini's office and the surveyor Chiodetti would be there later, when Esengrini returned from court...

Who else was in the office during that half hour? Had Esengrini left it for just a few moments, giving someone enough time to trace his signature onto a prepared letter?

Sciancalepre closed up the file, lost in thoughts that now had a sure focus. A little later the judge came back with some other people. Sciancalepre said nothing. He continued to think, starting involuntarily every now and again.

As he sat beside the judge on the road to M——, he whispered a name in his ear so that officer Pulito, who was driving, wouldn't hear it – or maybe just because he still feared being wrong.

The judge nodded. They didn't say anything else to each other, and for the rest of the journey they continued their silent scheming, eventually attaching a specific name to the findings Esengrini had dangled before the magistrates for a month.

As they entered the district prison for M——, the judge halted for a moment. He looked up at Sciancalepre. 'What if we're wrong? If this devil of a guy pulls out another name? If it's all been an infernal game?'

'We can expect anything,' Sciancalepre admitted, shaking his head. 'Even that mysterious man entering the game – the one who was in Esengrini's office on the day of the crime, according to the witness Rossinelli.'

'It's been nearly a month since we've seen each other,' Esengrini said to Sciancalepre after greeting the judge.

'We've moved Sciancalepre on to other things,' the judge explained, 'but he hasn't been sleeping on the job, and this morning he brought me a new key to the mystery, we hope.' So saying, he held out Signora Giulia's last letter for the lawyer to read.

'It is to my great fortune,' said Esengrini after reading it and reflecting, 'that Barsanti has always been a terrible guardian of his own correspondence. He loses one letter and for three years leaves another with the doorkeeper. But in addition to my mind, there's a hand keeping things in order here. A mysterious hand, scooping everything up. Now that we've got this letter, finding the jewellery isn't so important. But we shouldn't neglect anything.'

'Now,' the judge observed, 'I too have a request: I'd like to interrogate your typist and Demetrio Foletti in order to ascertain who was in your office on the Saturday morning when the letter with your forged signature went off to Barsanti.'

'The suggestion is a good one,' Esengrini admitted, 'but perhaps it's better to put it off; it could turn out to be useless. Let's try instead to reconstruct the crime, supposing, for example, that Demetrio Foletti had committed it. Just to check a possible theory.

'So: my wife, overcome by a serious Madame Bovary complex and emotionally needy, takes advantage of her weekly visits to our daughter at the convent school in order to escape the atmosphere of our town. On her way to Milan, she has the fatal encounter with Luciano Barsanti. After the first few meetings in various spots, Barsanti finds the right place in viale Premuda. They've already exchanged letters, as we know.

'My wife has the great idea of receiving letters through

Teresa Foletti, with the simple ruse of envelopes addressed by her in order to encourage the belief that they're coming from her daughter. Teresa believes in it, but her husband, who opens one of the initial letters – the second or the third – doesn't. Maybe more than one, but definitely the one which says that the little longed for nest is ready, and giving its address in viale Premuda. Like the true rep he is, Barsanti signs some of the love letters with his name and surname. Which means that Demetrio Foletti knows about my wife's liaison, knows the name of the lucky one and his exact address.

'He doesn't wait long before deciding on blackmail. It's easy to imagine how his desire, no doubt of long-standing, takes shape when he sees that the woman he once considered unattainable is within his grasp. With the mind of a gardener, he thinks that women, like flowers, yield their fragrance as often to the one who tends them as to the one who places them in the drawing-room; and sometimes more intensely to the one who tends them. One need only reach out one's hand to such a flower, using, if necessary, a little strength, and one has one's own share of the perfume… We can imagine the approach and the rejection. Demetrio, the family's right-hand man, goes in and out of the house at any hour; and my absences are continual and often last the entire day.

'Poor Giulia pays dearly for her evasion. At a certain point Demetrio becomes jealous, just like a husband, or even more so. And he dreams up the stratagem of sending the letter, purportedly from the husband who knows everything. He's used the system of tracing my signature a few other times, with my approval, and when signatures of little importance were necessary in my absence.

'Whether Barsanti keeps the letter to himself or whether he shows it to my wife, it must seem authentic. In both cases, and especially in the second one, it has the effect of halting the relationship. Foletti doesn't know that the affair was about to finish anyway, and that Barsanti is already sated with the perfume for which Foletti pants increasingly jealously.

'Barsanti was out of the picture, but he couldn't hope to take his place on that account. He had to realise that, the affair interrupted, his arguments for blackmail are weakened. But passion has no sense, and we have to imagine Demetrio overwhelmed and blinded by passion – and also by a desire for revenge. He came from a town near Bergamo, and started working as a gardener in my wife's house at the age of twenty-five. When I joined the Zaccagni-Lamberti house and transferred my offices there, I saw that he didn't have much to do in the garden, so I began to use him sometimes as an assistant and sometimes as a clerk. He went to the bank, to the post, to various offices. I saw that he was intelligent: when he had nothing else to do, he'd read copies of trials, study the statute book and literally immerse himself in criminology treatises. He ended up being my right-hand man, and I have to say that he has always behaved properly and served me willingly, occasionally managing to suggest theories for the defence that I had to reject only because they were too subtle. Demetrio is a relentless logician, gifted with imagination and intuition. Too much for a clerk or a gardener. He married the maid of my sister-in-law, who's dead. Teresa wasn't bad-looking in her youth but she's become an old woman in the last few years. We mustn't forget that she's ten years older than he is.

'At the time of the crime, Demetrio was only a little over forty, a lot younger than me: he considered himself a good-looking man, someone who'd begun to feel like something in between a clerk and my right-hand man. He could, in fact, aspire to my wife, all the more so after discovering that she'd already strayed from the straight and narrow.

'That Saturday he sends the letter and hopes the response will come via the usual means before Thursday. Thursday morning, when he sees that no letter with my wife's signature has arrived, he supposes Barsanti has not given any thought to the warning or the news he's received. It'll be necessary, therefore, to put pressure on Signora Giulia.

'He must already have suggested to my wife that morning that she shouldn't be going to Milan in the afternoon, and she would have been afraid. So she writes the letter that Sciancalepre found in viale Premuda a few days ago. It arrives in Milan a few days late, perhaps misdirected, and by that time Barsanti has already left for Rome. My wife would have gone out to post it at around ten that morning. Demetrio, sensing something's up, enters the house an hour later to press home the threats. He shoves her down the hall and she screams – Demetrio loses his cool and shuts her up for ever…

'The body is taken into the cellar via the internal staircase. The button I found under the wood on the cellar floor must have been torn from her dress when the killer dragged the body by the shoulders. The proximity of the cistern to the coach house is known only to Foletti; and he thinks he'll put the lifeless body there. The route from cellar to cistern is hidden from sight. And the house is empty except for the typist, who's in my office, which faces via Lamberti.

'I'm in court for a trial and won't be coming back before midday. Teresa is home and won't know anything. Foletti has

102

time to return to the house, take the suitcases, jumble some of my wife's clothes and linens into them and hide them in the cistern, not forgetting a purse or two. Inspired by Barsanti's letter, which he's intercepted, and in which the scrupulous rep discourages my wife from any such action, he fakes the flight.

'I haven't forgotten about the jewellery. When a wife leaves she always takes her jewellery with her. He knows, does Demetrio, that her jewellery constitutes a small fortune in itself. For this reason, he makes sure he doesn't put it in the suitcases, which neither he nor anyone else will ever unearth. He hides the jewellery, locked in a travelling case the size of your palm, by burying it in the greenhouse under a large urn used as a planter.'

The judge and Sciancalepre listened to the account without batting an eyelid. But at that point the judge exclaimed, 'So it's there, the jewellery!'

'It was,' Esengrini went on. 'A few months ago, when I was going back to the park every now and again at night, it was precisely as a result of having found the body that I was more than ever convinced I'd find the jewellery. Demetrio had followed all my searches. He'd noticed that I was looking underground for my wife in the park, and maybe he guessed that when I'd explored all other corners I'd find the cistern. But he needn't have worried: all the proof I found was against *me*. Evidently, I was the one with a reason to follow through with the killing – and I had no interest in stirring the law, which, fortunately for me, was dozing.

'The simulated flight and the missing body saved me from incrimination. The jewellery was the way he'd implicate me, by providing proof against me when necessary. When he realized

I was looking for it seriously and that I'd started to explore the greenhouse, he was forced to move it. He didn't want to lose it. One day, maybe ten or fifteen years hence, he'd sell it. But the moment might come when it would help him to put the blame on me, and deflect suspicion from himself. It would be better to have the jewellery found in my office.

'One night I noticed that a huge urn had been moved in the greenhouse. When I moved it, I found that the earth underneath it was freshly disturbed. Demetrio had been forced to take the jewellery out of the park. I hoped he'd taken it to his house. But he had the entire Sormani grounds at his disposal – and this is an important point – grounds to which he'd had free access for years, since the Sormani had entrusted him with looking after their few flowers. And that's why the shadow trying to kill my son-in-law came from the boundary wall between the villa Sormani and our park. Demetrio entered the grounds at night by the door in via Lamberti, to which he had the key, and went into the park to supervise my movements, while for my part I entered by the same door a bit later and went into the garden. As soon as he found out that my son-in-law wanted to turn the old coach house into a garage, and that he'd be exposing the paving stones by taking up the grass in order to put down cement, he knew the cistern would come to light, and my wife's tomb would be discovered. I knew it too, and prepared myself for some difficult days.

'It was more important than ever to find the jewellery and to know where it was hidden, because Demetrio could always use it against me. I felt I was in grave danger. I hid the letter with my forged signature in the Molinari file – S.I.R.C.E.; that is, in a place where it could be found easily upon my instructions, and I waited for further developments. Demetrio must have guessed that my son-in-law was planning to surprise the nocturnal visitor.'

'So,' the judge interrupted, 'your son-in-law told him that he was planning to catch the visitor, and Demetrio might have had the impression that Fumagalli was planning to act on his own.'

'For that reason,' Esengrini went on, 'he decided to surprise Fumagalli in the grounds, and to kill him without making any noise. When he was found with his skull fractured, who'd be accused if not me? My daughter knew I was walking around the park at night.'

'She knew it, and she's the one who saw you first,' Sciancalepre interrupted. 'And Demetrio also told Fumagalli, pointing out that he'd seen your shadow looking in the greenhouse with an electric light.'

'So we're all together now,' said Esengrini, 'and we can go on. If Fumagalli had been dead and they'd arrested me, of course I'd have had no choice but to deny it. It wouldn't have done to bring to light the body of my wife; it would have complicated my position to the point of absurdity. After the killing, the work on the garage would certainly not have gone forward. My daughter, horrified, would have left the villa and the grass would have continued to grow over that bit of the courtyard for who knows how long. The cistern would have kept its secret. But Demetrio could in any case have sent me to prison with the discovery of the jewellery. He could in fact have presented himself to the court as soon as my arrest was made public, to say that he felt it his duty to hand over a package I'd entrusted him to hide on my behalf. And he could still do that, not knowing that the two letters which nail him have been found.'

The judge was of the opinion that Foletti should be arrested immediately, since even if he played his trump card – presenting the jewellery and claiming that he'd had it from Esengrini or had found it in a hiding place – there was enough by now to convince him to admit to the crime. Sciancalepre promised to formulate a plan and put it to the judge. Esengrini returned once more to his cell, and the judge left.

The final act in the drama would feature Sciancalepre as protagonist. In the meantime, poor Barsanti was released, since by now he was out of the frame.

NINE

The entire city of M—— was convinced of Esengrini's guilt. Even the papers considered the case closed. Fumagalli and his wife decided to go away and stay in Switzerland for a few weeks to escape the journalists and paparazzi. Leaving their keys at Demetrio's house, they took off right after delivering their deposition to the investigating judge.

The conditions under which Sciancalepre had to act couldn't have been more favourable. Demetrio Foletti might suspect some manoeuvring on Esengrini's part in order to escape the two terrible charges against him. He might also have a rough idea of what Esengrini's line of defence was from the choice of witnesses summoned by the judge, and what was being prepared against him. The jewellery was definitely a serious problem for Foletti, since he would have sacrificed it just to save himself from prison and in order to implicate Esengrini definitively. Esengrini based his plan on these considerations and sketched it out to the judge, who gave Sciancalepre free rein.

Sciancalepre moved the very next day. He sent for Foletti to come to his office and kept more or less to this argument: 'Esengrini vehemently denies the charges, but all the proof is against him. We've even confiscated from his house the club he intended to kill his son-in-law with when he realized he was about to discover the cistern. Now we need to find the jewellery. Esengrini's office and apartment have been thoroughly searched without results and we have to consider, now, where the jewellery could be hidden in the old house – either in what was once his office or in some other spot in the wing he and his wife once occupied and which has now been vacant for some years. We'll carry out a long and painstaking search and you must help us, since you're more familiar with the place than any of us. We'll break down the walls, take up the floors…'

Foletti agreed immediately and the search began at around ten the next morning. Accompanied by Foletti, a sergeant and an officer, Sciancalepre opened the Fumagalli apartment with keys that had been left with Teresa; they also took the keys to Esengrini's old office and quarters.

They started their search in the office. At twelve-thirty the operation was suspended for lunch. Sciancalepre couldn't do without his pasta, but he advised Foletti to be back on the spot at two on the dot, and set off with his officers to eat. Foletti left the three of them in via Lamberti and went into his house opposite the palazzo Zaccagni-Lamberti.

The Commissario sent the sergeant home and, along with officer Pulito, he ran to the gate of the park, climbed over it, crossed the garden and went through the cellar into Esengrini's old apartment. Sciancalepre had taken the keys of the apartment with him as he'd left: he knew very well that if Foletti had swallowed the bait and wanted to come in and hide the jewellery there so it would be found later that afternoon, he had the means to do so.

In the entryway, two cupboards stood against opposite walls facing each other. Sciancalepre went into the one on the right and Pulito the one on the left. In order to enter the house and from there get into the apartment, Foletti would have to pass through that entryway.

Inside the cupboard, Sciancalepre calmed his panting after running and climbing over the gate. In the darkness his breath grew quiet, and he was about to crack open the cupboard door in order to get some fresh air when he heard a noise from the rusty hinges of the door that opened onto the courtyard. He waited a moment before bursting out of the cupboard and shouting to Pulito: 'Out!'

Demetrio Foletti stood in the middle of the hallway. Sciancalepre pointed the barrel of his revolver at his breast, while Pulito stationed himself behind him.

'Against the wall with your arms spread!' the Commissario commanded.

Pulito pushed Foletti along, taking hold of him by the neck and kneeing him in the back.

'Search his pockets,' Sciancalepre ordered Pulito, his gun still pointed at Foletti.

Pulito began with Foletti's jacket pockets, throwing everything he found to the ground: a handkerchief, a large jackknife, a box of matches. He then went through the trouser pockets, pulling out a heavy sack. Sciancalepre signalled for Pulito to pass him the sack.

He felt it, untied it, and folded down the sides: a blaze of glittering diamonds. Signora Giulia's jewellery. He took a pin between two fingers and held it up to examine it. He'd seen it so many times at the edge of her collar, on her breast! He put it back and took out a strand of pearls coiled between the gold and the diamonds, dangling it in front of them for a moment before squeezing it and letting it fall back into the sack. It was warm. After having been warmed so many times against the soft neck of Signora Giulia, it had now, inside Demetrio's pocket, absorbed the heat of a killer. He put the sack of jewellery in his own pocket and calmly turned to Foletti.

'Show me the exact spot where you killed her.'

Foletti had turned round but Pulito kept him against the wall, his arms spread.

'Let him go,' ordered Sciancalepre, having stationed himself at the door leading out to the courtyard. He turned again to Foletti. 'Walk!' he said loudly.

Foletti walked to the end of the hallway and turned round, wringing his hands and crying out, 'It's not true! It's not true!'

'Killer!' Sciancalepre shouted. 'We found the letter you forged and another from Signora Giulia to Barsanti accusing you. Where were you going with the jewellery? And where have you been keeping it until now?'

Foletti remained with his face to the door. His entire body began to tremble.

'Where did you kill her!' Sciancalepre screamed once more.

Foletti nearly fainted. Sciancalepre and Pulito carried him into the drawing-room, put him in a chair and sat on either side of him. When he came to, the Commissario demanded, 'Well? Tell me where you were going with this sack in your pocket!'

'Signor Commissario, I'm innocent! I haven't killed anyone. The killer is him, Esengrini. And now I'll show you how.'

'The day Signora Giulia disappeared,' he began, 'I left the office just after midday, as soon as Esengrini got back from court. His typist had gone a few minutes before. Signora

Giulia must still have been in the house, because I heard a door shut in the apartment. My wife had left about half an hour earlier, having finished her work. The lawyer stayed in his office and I went home. About half an hour later I saw Esengrini go out and I knew that he had set off to tell you about the signora's disappearance. After a few days of doubt I became certain that the lawyer had killed his wife and hidden her body in the house or garden. I looked for a long time, all over the park, and once I saw Esengrini going over the grounds with an Alsatian; I persuaded myself that far from looking for his wife – he knew very well where she was – he was actually trying to ascertain whether a dog could have discovered her burial place. I noticed that he halted with the dog in the clearing in front of the coach house with particular insistence, and I became suspicious that it was actually there that he'd buried Signora Giulia, but in such a way that not even a fox could have sniffed her out. I recalled that under the courtyard there was a cistern, hermetically sealed by a stone sunk into it.

'A few days had passed since the disappearance and there'd been some rain, so it wasn't possible for the dog to follow a scent, even less so since Esengrini would not have dragged the body, but carried it over his shoulders after opening the manhole and then dropped the body into it. He must have gone down after the body to drag it into a corner of the cistern, where he probably also put down the suitcases. Only the floods, later, must have made them float up to the surface where they could be seen from the opening. Without the floods, perhaps the builders would never have discovered the body.'

'But,' the Commissario interrupted, 'when did you become certain about all this?'

'A few days afterwards, on a day when Esengrini was in Milan and I went to lift the lid on the cistern. I looked inside with an electric light and saw everything.'

'So why didn't you come to me with your discovery?'

'Because I was afraid of being charged with the crime. I had more than once made the signora aware that I, too, was a man, and she might have told her lover in Milan that I was trying it on with her. Maybe she'd left some trace – I don't know – a confidence to a friend, a letter, a diary entry that indicated something. And then, since I'm innocent, it suited me that the signora should be considered to have fled, or to have ended up who knows where. But perhaps you didn't know she had a lover in Milan?'

'Come on! But how did *you* know? And all these things – why did you never come and tell me, at least in the past few days since Esengrini was arrested?'

'I knew she had a lover because she had him write to my house. I discovered it by opening some of the letters without my wife's knowledge, and then closing them carefully so the signora wouldn't notice. My wife would have thought they were letters from Signorina Emilia. I didn't say a thing to her; but I read some and it seemed to me that Signora Giulia had a lover near where she went every Thursday, in viale Premuda: some Barsanti. When I realized this, I got it into my head that Signora Giulia was an unsatisfied woman, and that if she had a thing going with this Barsanti, maybe there was a little hope for me, too. I let her know what I was thinking, but there was nothing in it for me apart from scorn – and little gifts of money

112

to keep me sweet. My little whim, a bit of nothing, really, started there – with that scorn – and ended up trapping her, with some success, actually.'

'What do you mean?'

'Nothing important – just so… to keep me happy. But I had to accept that she loved Barsanti, and there was nothing I could do about it.'

'But how did Esengrini know about Barsanti?'

'I don't know. He probably knew more about all of this than me, to act as he did. If he killed her, he had to have a reason, something that drove him to it.'

Sciancalepre cut him off. 'Let's get to the jewellery.'

'I didn't know that the jewellery was missing. Or rather… that Esengrini had hidden it without putting it in the suitcases, in order to make it seem like she'd fled. I realized what had happened a year later. One morning when I went into the greenhouse, I saw that a large vase of lemons had been moved. It was chance, since the vase was behind some others. Surprised, I moved it to one side and saw that the earth underneath it had been disturbed. I thought an animal, maybe a mole, had been making a burrow. I took up a hoe and immediately struck it against a metal box. It was the little case in which the signora kept her jewellery. Inside, in a sack, the same one you have in your pocket now, were her jewels. I thought if Esengrini had moved them from some initial hiding place, there had to be a reason.

'I can tell you that one day while I was talking to Signora Giulia and trying to get her to give in, it occurred to me that her husband, who'd tiptoed from his office, must have caught on. He said nothing; on the contrary, from then on, he treated

113

me with the utmost kindness. That episode, however, must have given him the idea of fingering me as the murderer. His daughter, Signorina Emilia, didn't look him in the eye any more. One day soon, the body would be discovered, and Esengrini, having planned all this ahead of time, was preparing evidence against me.'

'Ah, so that's how it is? And the letter to Barsanti, you never wrote it, by tracing over Esengrini's signature? We have the letter! And the document with the original signature! It's all over, my good man. It's time you told us the truth.'

'What letter! What signature? I never wrote any letter.'

'But you knew Barsanti's address?'

'Yes, I read it in one of his letters to the signora, the one where he said he'd found a pied-à-terre at viale Premuda, n. XY.'

'There you go!'

'But why should I have written to him?'

'Because you were jealous. To intimidate him. And you wrote to him on Esengrini's letterhead, with his signature, tracing it against the window from a sheet underneath that had his true signature on it. You can't deny it: we have the evidence!'

'As far as I'm concerned, if what you say is true, it's evidence against Esengrini. Having decided to kill his wife, he prepared all the evidence against me. In fact, he could have traced over his own signature. And also, doesn't it say something to you that he saved those documents so carefully for three years?'

'So why's the jewellery in your pocket?'

'I was coming to that, Signor Commissario. When I found the jewellery under the vase in the greenhouse, I knew it had been put there on purpose. In fact, only I could have hidden it there. Wasn't I the gardener? I took it away and hid it somewhere else.'

'Where?'

'On top of a tree. See that cedar over there? Halfway up the trunk, you can still see the little jewellery case secured to the top of a branch by four nails. Only by cutting down that tree, which is two hundred years old and will live for another four hundred, could someone have discovered the jewellery.

'Esengrini noticed that I'd removed the jewellery. A few months later he checked under the vase, and saw that the little box was no longer there. So he knew that I'd found him out, and thinking that I'd simply moved it somewhere else he patiently began looking for it. Every day I found some sign of his nighttime searches. He was set on looking at the ground, while the jewellery was up in the air! I began to think that without that particular means of accusing me, Esengrini could simply find others in order to nail me. But I felt fairly calm: the courts seemed to have archived the case.

'Years went by, and finally Signorina Emilia got married and her father moved out of the house. Fearing that I'd hidden the jewellery badly and that Fumagalli would find it some day or other, he started looking again. He even used a plumb line: I'm sure of it, because one day he had a specialist come to the office and he pretended just to be curious, asking him how to use one of those cords with lead on it. During moonlit nights, he'd come to the park and spend an hour or so looking.

'It was in this way that Fumagalli and Emilia noticed their nocturnal visitor and tried to catch him. Esengrini didn't suspect it, and the night he saw his son-in-law walking round the park he tried to kill him with the club, thinking that Fumagalli

115

was alone. If there hadn't been any gunshots, he'd be answering for two murders now. And his decision to kill his son-in-law in that way wasn't a rash one. If the club had struck home, who would they have accused? Certainly not him. Some thief, or, actually, probably me. However, the work adapting the garage from the old coach house would have been halted and Signora Giulia's grave would never have come to light. Signora Emilia would definitely have left this house, where both her mother and her husband had mysteriously been murdered. Everything would surely have remained in the dark for ever.'

Sciancalepre was stunned. Foletti's version was no worse than Esengrini's and certainly just as plausible. In any case, thinking he could at least accuse Foletti of stealing the jewels, he asked, 'So where were you going with the jewellery?'

'Yesterday I climbed up the tree to get it after you spoke to me about the search, and I stuffed it in my pocket. I was going to put it up the drawing-room chimney, and you'd have found it there because I would have seen to it that you did. It would have constituted decisive proof against Esengrini. Actually, he might have hidden it in that spot on the day of the murder, since when I found it the little box was covered with soot. Since I was sure that Esengrini had committed the murder, I felt I was collaborating with the law by piecing together the evidence against him. The status quo, as they say.'

Sciancalepre wasn't sure what to do, but he declared Foletti under arrest anyway and took him into custody. He then phoned the investigating judge who hurried to M——, where he took down the gardener's long deposition.

Over the following days Sciancalepre challenged Esengrini with it. Esengrini listened calmly, nodding his head continuously. Asked by the judge what objections he might raise, he responded: 'None. It's a good theory. Except that it can so easily be overturned. Foletti admits to having solicited the favours of my wife: there's your motive for the killing. Seized by a jealous passion, he put himself in my shoes as the cuckold and wrote the threatening letter to Barsanti. He forged my signature on it, tracing it from the document found on my table. It's easy for him to say that I fabricated that letter in order to furnish advance proof against him. However, I'd have needed to know about his passion for my wife! And it doesn't follow that I did, even if he says so.

'The jewellery made quite a journey! Up the chimney – then, with the coming autumn making him fear that the fires would burn the little metal box and it would all fall down onto the hearth, he buried it in the greenhouse. Seeing that I was searching diligently in the grounds, even with a plumb line, he thought to put it in the cedar where I certainly wouldn't be climbing. The hiding place was perfect since that cedar is very dense and never loses its foliage.'

'Now then,' the judge asked, 'you admit that your wife was killed in your house and buried in the cistern, and that the signs of her flight were faked?'

'I'm sure of it. And I don't see how anyone besides Demetrio Foletti could be accused of the crime.'

Having presented the lawyer's contradictions to Foletti and obtained from him the same admissions, and, naturally, having put the counter-accusations to Esengrini, the judge resorted to a confrontation.

■

The confrontation took place in the prison cells of T——
where the two detainees had been transferred. It was less dramatic than expected. When the gardener was brought into the
room where the lawyer already stood before the judge and the
clerk, he greeted the magistrate correctly. Then, to Esengrini:
'*Buongiorno*, Signor Esengrini,' to which the lawyer responded,
'Hello, Demetrio.'

Esengrini's depositions were read out to him. Asked if he
would confirm them, he answered, 'From the first word to the
last.'

'Therefore,' the judge concluded, 'you indicate Demetrio
Foletti, present here, as the killer of your wife.'

'Demetrio Foletti is my wife's murderer,' the lawyer confirmed.

Then Foletti's depositions were read out to him, and he, too,
confirmed them. When he was asked who had committed the
murder, he answered, indicting Esengrini: 'The lawyer.'

The judge had to acknowledge that apart from the reciprocal accusations, there was no other exchange between the two
detainees except on the matter of the letter to Barsanti.

'How often,' Esengrini asked Foletti, 'did you copy my signature with my permission on requests, citations, even bills, by
tracing over a document held against the window?'

'Countless times, Signor Esengrini. But not on the letter to
Barsanti, which I never typed out.'

'So then, would I have traced my own signature!?'

'Of course, Signor Esengrini! Who else would have? Only
you had a motive for creating a document with which you could
accuse me.'

'Bravo. But explain this: once I sent that letter to Barsanti,
how could I hope to come into possession of it again, in order

to save it as proof against you? You know – or perhaps you don't – that the letter was returned to me by sheer coincidence? That it was found years later in Milan, inside a piece of furniture sold at auction?'

'That's as may be. But it could also be that you imagined Barsanti would take greater care with the letters he received. And since Barsanti was going to be found one day or another, you could have asked him to produce the letter so that you could deny having written it, claiming I'd written it instead, having forged your signature. And that's exactly what you did do, using a document lying around in your office that day. The game was set, even without the miraculous recovery of the letter.'

'Capital theory!' returned the lawyer. 'One can't deny it. Except that it's also possible things happened as I said.'

Given that further confrontation was pointless, the judge closed proceedings and sent the detainees back to their cells.

But he put to himself a difficult question: which of the two should he send to trial at the court of assizes? Should he send them both back? One of them was surely innocent, and just as surely the other one was guilty. Weighing the evidence over and over, the judge found the scales equally balanced. He ended up sending them both back to trial charged as accomplices to murder and attempted murder. Knowing, however, that they would both be acquitted.

TEN

The trial was unspectacular. Imperturbable, the two accused repeated their parallel declarations point for point. The one was just as contented as the other with the official defenders, who both got away at the close of the hearing with addresses of only five minutes each. The same public prosecutor had requested the acquittal of both men due to insufficient proof, since he was unable to demonstrate any plot or cooperation whatsoever between them in the execution of the crimes specified in the charge: the murder of Giulia Zaccagni-Lamberti, and the attempted murder of Carlo Fumagalli.

On the day of the trial, Sciancalepre and the investigating judge, who had conducted the case, were in the city in order to interrogate a detainee on remand. Their duty executed, they were walking down the administrative corridor just as Esengrini and Foletti entered the registry office to collect their valuables and complete the final bureaucratic formalities of their imprisonment.

'They're leaving,' said the judge, his hand on Sciancalepre's arm. 'Going home.'

A short time later they saw them head for the exit, accompanied by a guard. The judge and Sciancalepre followed behind, careful not to overtake them.

Once through the door, the lawyer and Foletti turned left along the wall of the prison towards the city centre. The judge and the Commissario kept them within eyesight while slowly walking along the pavement, side by side. Without a doubt they were talking, but not looking at one another, their words lost in the din of the traffic.

'I'd give ten years of my life,' said Sciancalepre, 'to hear what they're saying to each other.'

When they reached the end of the prison wall, Esengrini and Foletti stopped for a moment. Then, like two duellists turning their backs and measuring the prescribed distance, they turned in opposite directions, one to the right, the other to the left, still walking in step.

—

Did you know?

Initially published in 1962 as a serial in a Swiss local newspaper, *The Disappearance of Signora Giulia* was the first of Piero Chiara's novels to appear in print, although he had published a number of novels by the time it was made available in book form in 1970. Chiara later revealed the town of M——, where the story unfolds, to be inspired by Porto Ceresio on Lake Lugano, close to the border with Switzerland. The name of the book's detective, Sciancalepre, comically suggests 'lame hare' in Italian.

It was perhaps the dramatic setting of Chiara's childhood – on the picturesque shores of the Italian lakes – that helped to lend such a distinctly cinematic quality to his writing, full of chiaroscuro scenery and colourful characters. Chiara was quite a character himself, and worked as a court employee, journalist and teacher before retiring early to dedicate himself to writing. A politically engaged man, he was forced to flee to Switzerland in 1944 after the Fascist authorities issued a warrant for his arrest (rumour has it that he had installed a bust of Mussolini in the dock of his local courtroom).

One of Italy's most celebrated post-war writers, Chiara wrote novels, short stories and poetry, which won him more than a dozen literary prizes, and were adapted into countless films and TV series. He even took to starring in some of these himself, playing the role of magistrate in the TV adaptation of *The Disappearance of Signora Giulia*. The Premio Chiara has since been established in Italy as an annual literary prize that rewards writers of short stories.

So, where do you go from here?

If you'd like another slice of classic Italian crime, look no further than Augusto De Angelis's intensely dramatic **The Murdered Banker** – marking the brilliant debut of the sophisticated Milanese sleuth, Inspector De Vincenzi.

If you'd prefer something completely different we can recommend Leo Perutz's **The Master of the Day of Judgment** – a spine-tingling, hallucinatory Conan-Doylesque mystery set in Austro-Hungarian Vienna.

AVAILABLE AND COMING SOON FROM PUSHKIN VERTIGO

Augusto De Angelis

The Murdered Banker
The Mystery of the Three Orchids
The Hotel of the Three Roses

Boileau-Narcejac

Vertigo
She Who Was No More

Piero Chiara

The Disappearance of Signora Giulia

Martin Holmén

Clinch

Alexander Lernet-Holenia

I Was Jack Mortimer

Leo Perutz

Master of the Day of Judgment
Little Apple
St Peter's Snow

Soji Shimada

The Tokyo Zodiac Murders